IRON FIST KEEP

PROPHECY OF AXAIN, BOOK 2

STEVEN ATWOOD

ISBN 13: 9781949788068

Published by Dragons & Lasers Press

Carrollton, GA 30116

CHAPTER 1

The Test

*W*here *is that bastard?* Galin V of Ravenward thought as he hid behind a stack of boxes in the small room. His blue eyes looked out the door into the hallway, looking for the guard to pass. He ran his fingers through his shoulder-length brown hair. It had to be there, right? The Vulwin Elf merchant told them that she sold the Ointment of Healing to the mage, the only remedy that could save Ellis. Galin bit his lip. He was more concerned about passing his test and nearly let his lifelong friend die, which still may happen. "It's clear," he whispered towards the window behind him.

"Okay," Jena whispered. Her long blond hair fell over her face as she crawled through the tiny wooden window. Her blue eyes softened as she knelt next to

Galin. Pushing her hair over a shoulder, she exposed the golden full moon tattooed on her neck. "Where are we?"

Galin swallowed as Jena got close. His hand yearned for her touch, but he had to concentrate. He had to save Ellis. The small room had stacks of boxes, with no furniture in sight. There was a broom in a corner, along with a bucket hanging from a peg on the wall. "Not sure, a storeroom of some kind." He rose to his feet. "That guard hasn't come back in a while. Should be clear now."

"I don't know," Jena said as she moved next to him.

He pressed against the wall, right next to the door. That guard had to come back, right? Then they could take him out—or her, or it, or whatever it was—and find the ointment. "How much time do we have?"

Jena's eyes were puffy. "I'm not sure. I never tried to cure the devil's infection before. We need to hurry."

Galin nodded. Should they wait for the guard to come back around? What if he didn't come back until later, much later? Yeah, they had to hunt him down. He drew his sword. The hilt was covered with tightly wound leather strips and there was a dragon etched on the blade. It glistened in the light, just like when his adoptive father had given it to him over eighteen months ago. His grip tightened as he stepped into the hallway.

A sconce was mounted on the far wall with a lit torch illuminating the hallway. The moisture on the oak walls glistened in the torchlight. Doors at both ends were closed, but the doorway on the opposite wall was open.

Galin blinked. *There, the guard must be in there.* He looked back at Jena and pointed his sword towards the open door.

She nodded.

He moved across the hallway and crept along the wall towards the door. Galin's soft leather boots were silent on the flagstone floor. He stepped heel to toe, just like Brock Feran taught him to stalk prey in Sarun Grove. Galin stopped just before the door and looked back at Jena. He wouldn't lose her like he did his adoptive mother; never.

Jena drew her short sword and motioned Galin towards the door.

Galin swallowed. They had to save Ellis. He held up his fingers and start to count down.

Five.

His stomach twisted.

Four.

Jena moved closer to Galin. Her eyes narrowed.

Three.

Galin's grip on his sword tightened.

Two.

He edged towards the door.

One.

Galin rushed inside the room, with Jena close behind him. No guard. The sconces on the walls were lit. The guard's simple desk and bed were unoccupied. Nothing. "We should look around. It may be here." Along the far wooden wall was an empty, primitive bookcase. There was an open crate next to the soiled bed. He moved towards the crate. "I'll check this one out."

Jena grimaced. "Should we stay here that long? There wouldn't be a valuable magic item here, would there?"

Galin shrugged. "Maybe they wanted thieves to think that. Besides, I won't be long." He began to rummage through the crate. As he moved the filthy clothes around, the odor of pig feces stung his nostrils. His eyes began to water as he pulled his head back from the crate. "This stuff stinks."

Jena screamed.

Galin whirled around and his heart almost stopped as he saw Jena slump to the floor with a dagger stuck in her back.

A goblin with green skin wearing a red robe pulled his dagger out of her back. "Foolish child." His red eyes shined in the torchlight. "Anyone who trespasses in this tower pays with their life."

Even the gods themselves couldn't tear his eyes away from Jena's bleeding, crumpled body lying on the floor. His face reddened. "You killed her."

The goblin smiled. "Don't worry, you'll join her soon enough." He reached into his robe and pulled out a wand. "How does boiling your blood inside you sound?"

A tingle itched Galin's heart. The more enraged he got, the more the tingle spread throughout his chest. Tiny electrical arcs began to dance across his skin. His eyes began to glow. The tiny arcs grew bigger as they engulfed his sword.

The goblin stepped back. "What sorcery is this?" He raised his wand.

"No!" Galin charged at the goblin with his sword raised. As he swung his sword at the goblin's head, the electrical arcs jumped from his sword to the goblin. As the sword slashed his skin, the goblin screamed as his flesh smoldered. A small vial fell from his burning robes, breaking on the flagstone floor. Galin's eyes widened as he saw the contents spill out onto the floor.

He looked over at Jena. He'd lost her, just like he'd lost Sally Feran, his adoptive mother. The more he looked at her, the more enraged he got. The arcs dancing across his body turned red. The unmistakable smell of burning flesh invaded his nostrils. It wasn't the goblin's flesh; no, it was his own. Pain, pain seared through his body as he collapsed to the floor. Galin was determined to make sure the last thing he saw was Jena's beautiful face. Was this it?

"You failed again!" screamed a male voice.

The pain vanished from Galin. As the mage's warehouse vanished. Galin sighed as the small, stone-walled room came into focus. A short, male Snow Elf with very short white hair and ghastly, wrinkled skin showing his age stood there. His cold blue eyes bore right through Galin's confidence.

"Nyna, please. I can do it."

Jena shook her head as she got up off the floor. "My head spins every time I do that."

Nyna glared at her. "You're only here because Sumia insisted, like the other one."

The door flew open. "When can we eat? I'm starving," said a stout young man with short black hair and hazel eyes. He wore a tan tunic with red pants. He smiled.

Galin stared at Ellis. "Ellis, please, this is important."

Jena rolled her eyes. "When is he *not* hungry?"

Nyna snapped his fingers. "Galin, to my office now." He stormed out of the small room.

"How many times am I going to fail that test?" Galin moved over to Jena and reached for her hand. His eyes sagged as he looked at her. "Father will be so disappointed in me."

"We don't need that old fool," Ellis said. "We're just wasting time here anyway."

Jena frowned. "Ellis, this is important to Galin."

"I'll meet you in the dining hall," Galin said.

Jena kissed him. "Okay."

Is Ellis right? Galin thought as he left the Test Chamber.

AFTER A FEW MINUTES of navigating through the hallways of Tadus School of Magic, Galin arrived at the faculty wing. The long hallway had at least thirty doors, fifteen on both sides, leading to the instructors' offices. Each door not only had a nameplate, but it also had various shapes and symbols of the disciplines they followed. A golden dragon breathing fire on a rock surrounded by a golden circlet decorated Nyna's door. Galin sighed as he opened it.

Nyna sat behind an elaborate maple desk. On the back wall was a bookcase filled with well-used tomes and scroll cases. A torch that never burns out was in the sconce on the wall. "Sit down, Galin."

Galin sat down in the rickety wooden chair in front of Nyna's desk. "I'm sorry, I—"

Nyna held up his hand, silencing Galin. "No more of that, just listen to me. You've failed your final exam twice. I know that the other students study for years and you—you can't wait that long." Nyna lowered his voice. "I know you're the one the Darkstrider prophecy speaks of, but you'll destroy yourself if you don't control it. If you fail here, you could never return to learn more."

"Who says I need to?" Galin asked.

"You use dragon magic and you must learn from a real dragon master, not a Snow Elf who happens to know a little dragon magic," Nyna said. "Your power will continue to grow, as well as the risk of using it. You've got to come back."

Galin nodded. "I understand."

Nyna shook his head. "No, you don't. There is one variable that causes you to fail every test. It is an undeniable fact."

"What is it?"

Nyna's eyes narrowed. "That human female. The one you're always fawning over. Every time something happens to her you forget everything I've taught you, endangering yourself and everyone around you."

Galin swallowed. "I love her. We're going to get married."

"No, you can't do that until you're king," Nyna said. "If something happens to her, or the Darkstriders capture her—or worse—your rage will engulf you. You will not only kill your enemies but yourself and everyone around you. As a prince, you have to think of others before yourself."

"But—what do I tell her?" Galin asked.

Nyna rubbed his chin. "Tell her that you need to wait because—because you want her to become your queen, not just a revolutionary's wife." He motioned Galin to the door. "Now go, and let me get back to my studies."

Galin nodded and headed out the door. *What am I going to tell Jena?*

GALIN MADE his way to the Dining Hall. The great room had three long tables that nearly stretched from one end to the other. The walls were decorated with paintings of the gods, great battles, and the long and dark history of Tadus School of Magic. The numerous images told the story of how the school became a neutral magic school, training those who study light, dark, and neutral magic. It was a place where enemies were friends while they studied magic. There were few humans that attended the school. The student population consisted of Gnomes, Dwarves, Snow Elves, Mountain Elves, and many Dark Elves. There were only twenty or so human students, all of which were female.

Galin searched the sea of students for Jena and Ellis. His eyes jumped from table to table, section to section, until he saw Jena's glowing face. How could he do what Nyna told him he must do? He loved Jena, but—but he'd die without her. Fulfilling the prophecy without Jena at his side would not be honorable, it would be stale and sorrowful. No, he needed Jena to survive. He needed Jena to love him. She was his strength. Maybe he could just delay things a little until he got a handle on things. Maybe?

Jena smiled as she waved Galin over.

Galin beamed as he moved towards them.

Ellis popped a piece of bread into his mouth. "What did the old bag have to say this time?"

As Galin sat down, a flying brown fairy floated above him. "What do you want for dinner, Galin?"

"Chicken and potatoes, please," Galin said.

The fairy snapped her fingers and a plate appeared. "Enjoy," she said as she flew towards another student.

The baked chicken was covered in a meat gravy crowned with parsley. The steaming mashed potatoes were right next to the beans fried in onions. The aroma called to Galin's stomach. "I wish I could do that," Galin said.

Jena smiled at Galin. "What did Nyna say?"

Galin cut off a piece of chicken, tossing it in his mouth. "Oh, this is good."

"Galin?"

Ellis snickered. "He's got his priorities right, Jena. Eat first, then talk."

Galin looked into her soft blue eyes. What should he tell her? "I am in danger of failing and I must pass."

"Why do you care?" Ellis asked. "Like I've said over the past year and a half, you don't need them. You've got a handle on it now."

Galin shook his head. "Not really. He also said my power will continue to grow and I will need to eventually train under a dragon master."

"You're nuts," Ellis said as he tossed a piece of steak into his mouth.

"He's been right before," Jena said. "Maybe you should listen to him."

She doesn't know what she's asking, Galin thought. "I—"

"I've heard of you," a Dark Elf female said as she pointed at Galin. "You're the reason my mother was killed."

A red-haired gnome grabbed her hand. "Don't, they'll punish you."

She broke away from the short creature. "I don't care."

"I had nothing to do with it," Galin said as he glared at her.

Ellis rolled his eyes. "Oh, please, and who are you, *exactly?*"

"I'm Chalia, daughter of Beldroth," said the long-haired Dark Elf. Her black hair had a golden stripe running through it.

Galin saw that the average-built Dark Elf

attempted to act physically tough but knew her real strength was not in her muscles, rather in her power. "Look, Chalia, I've never heard of Beldroth. I had nothing to do with your mother's death. Please, leave us be."

Chalia reached into her robes and pulled out a platinum ball. It laid flat in the palm of her hand and her eyes stared right at Galin. "Stein nim tsak srot."

Galin drew his sword. "I'm warning you."

Chalia's eyes narrowed. "Stein nim tsak srot."

"I hate these people," Ellis said. He stood up and threw a piece of pie at Chalia.

A smile cracked across Chalia's face. "Stein—" The blueberry pie hit Chalia square in the face. She dropped the platinum ball and it rolled underneath the table. She glared at Ellis. "You!" She pushed aside a dwarf and took his bowl of potatoes and threw it at Ellis.

He saw it coming and ducked. "You missed." He started to laugh.

Chalia's mouth uttered a few inaudible words.

The potatoes rose up from the broken bowl behind Ellis. It flew around his head and hit him square in the face.

Jena giggled.

Galin laughed.

Ellis frowned.

Chalia laughed, as if the potatoes broke the tension.

The plates of food rose from the plates in front of Chalia and slammed into her face. Her dark eyes glared through the gravy running down her face.

"Don't look at me, I didn't do it," Galin said. "I—" Chicken soup splashed on his face.

The room erupted in laughter. Food began to fly across the room, hitting everyone in its path. No one was safe and everyone was guilty.

"You people are nuts!" Ellis said as he ducked behind the table. "They don't even have to use their hands to have a food fight."

Jena dodged a flying chocolate mousse. "You'd just use it to steal stuff."

Ellis grinned. "Of course."

"Let's get out here!" Galin said. As he stood up, a flying bowl of grits dumped its contents in his hair. It was rolling down his face. "Great."

Chalia glared at Galin. "I'll see you again. I—" An apple pie hit her in the face.

"Stop!" Nyna yelled from the doorway. He made an arm motion and all the food disappeared.

Galin looked down at his clothes. All the chocolate, grits, and who knew whatever else was gone. All that was left in the room were the amazed apprentices. "Nyna, I—"

Nyna held up his hand, silencing Galin. "Everyone, go back to your dormitory." He pointed at Galin, Jena, and Ellis. "You three, come with me."

"Let's go," Galin said. They followed Nyna out the door.

CHAPTER 2

Artis the Black

rtis the Black stared out his office window onto the budding city of Drusas. He couldn't be considered a simple or humble man. The governor's office was decorated with paintings, statuettes, and rare books that used to belong to the wealthiest noblemen in the kingdom of Axain. The dead had no use for such antiquities. A group of green Feral Orcs armed with two hand axes wearing chainmail armor marched through the city square. *A city? Really? More like a village pretending to be a city.* He ran his fingers through his shoulder-length brown hair. His green eyes sagged as the Feral Orcs were harassing a mother carrying a baby, *again.* "They lack any honor; even the Dark Elf Knights have that." He sat down behind the polished mahogany desk into his black-cushioned chair.

"What can we do about it?" Lena Blunt asked.

Artis turned around and looked at his assistant. "We control it. What else do we need?"

Lena brushed her light-brown hair from her brown eyes. "How?"

"By having what they want, what else? Ever since Shania failed her mission, Tanyl has become desperate. He's convinced that this—prince, is the prophesied king."

Her thin body slid into the brown-cushioned chair across from his desk. "Really?" She looked away from him. "Maybe—maybe we should help him."

Artis shook his head. "No, even if it is true, their forces would crush any army that he could possible raise."

A woman screamed just outside his window.

Artis didn't even flinch. "That's the only way to make that stop."

"Are you sure?"

"Look, after the Darkstriders invaded, I had to make some hard choices. I could've joined that failed rebellion or tried to make things better for everyone," Artis said. "I executed the rebellion leaders for the good of the people, nothing more."

Lena frowned. "Before the war, you were just a squire, on your way out of the service."

Artis nodded. "True, I have ascended in status."

"And wealth," Lena said. "How will hiring Tasar help us? I mean, don't you have enough gold and power?"

"No," Artis said, "I don't. Imagine, Lena, what I could do with control everything east of the Wailing Mountains, including the Ithsein province? If we give them no reason to interfere with our affairs, they won't." He sniffed. "Why would they bother?"

Lena walked over to the window. "It's only going to get worse under them. You know the rumors about what they're doing on Etrana. Why wouldn't they do the same thing here?"

Artis felt the hair rising on the back of his neck. He shook his head. "That's why we've given them no reason to use those…tactics."

Lena raised her eyebrows. "What if you're wrong?"

He grunted. Could he be throwing away the one chance to be free from the Darkstriders? No, no one could raise and train an army big enough to push them to their side of the Fadyhl Waters. Even if one was raised, Staerdale Castle only fell one time and that was when the Darkstriders took it. No, there was no way any boy king could change any of it. But, what if he did? It was obvious. He'd be strung up like the traitor that he was, but he wouldn't go alone. "I'm not, so don't worry about. Besides, I'm not the only one who would be…punished if the prophecy does come true."

Knock. Knock. Knock.

Lena rose from her chair. "I'll get it."

Artis swallowed.

Lena opened the oak door. The Dark Elf with deep-blue skin and lifeless, black eyes smiled. "Please come in," Lena said.

His flowing red robe with purple trim nearly

reached all the way to the floor. His should-length black hair was pulled back into a ponytail. He smiled. "This is the first time I've been requested by a governor." He slid into the cushioned chair next to the one Lena had sat in.

Artis smiled. If he went through with this, there was no turning back. He had to be sure. What if he failed?

"How was your trip, Tasar?" Lena asked as she sat down.

Tasar yawned. "Uneventful." His eyes narrowed. "But, I didn't cross the Wailing Mountains for conversation."

"You're right," Artis said. "I asked you here for a job." That was it. There was no turning back now. "My problem is that ever since Shania failed to grab the prince, my city has been constantly overrun by *your* Feral Orcs."

Tasar frowned. "I'm not a Darkstrider. They're not *my* orcs."

Artis waved him off. "Whatever. Anyway, I need them to leave us alone."

"I don't see how I can help you," Tasar said as he started to stand up.

Lena grabbed his arm. "Please, hear him out."

"Fine," he said as he sat back down. "Since I'm not on the council or even in the chain of command—or even in the Darkstriders—I can't just tell them to go away."

Artis leaned toward Tasar. "But you can remove the reason for them being here in the first place."

Tasar leaned back into his chair. "Go on."

"Tanyl believes Prince Galin V is the boy king your prophecy talks about. I want you to—"

"You want me to kill him so you can take credit for it," Tasar finished. "He would be very grateful. In fact, he may just make you a..." His eyes grew big. "You could be the first human Darkstrider noble." His lips twisted. "Very nice."

Artis sighed. "It has to be made to look like an accident or something."

"Why?" Tasar asked. "If you bring Tanyl his head, it'll be over."

Lena shook her head. "No, it wouldn't."

"We can't make a martyr out of him either," Artis said. He reached down into a drawer in his desk and pulled out a small chest. "How much?"

Tasar rose and walked over to the window. "All of this will be yours? Maybe even into Ithsein itself?" He saw the bustle of the square and smiled.

Artis grinned. "Hopefully."

"Why? Why are you doing this? If he is the prophesied one, he could free your people," Tasar said.

"They can't win, even if it is true," Artis said. "Will you take the job?"

Tasar rubbed his hands together. "Sure, I'll take it. The question is, can you afford me?"

Artis settled into his chair. "How much?"

"I'll do it for 300,000 crowns, and I want half before I move an inch." Tasar grinned as Artis' face turned red. "Also, if I fail, you keep the remainder. When I bring you his head—after his accident, of course—I want the last 150,000 crowns."

Artis jumped to his feet. "Three hundred thousand!? That's outrageous. I can get a local to do the job for a fraction of that price."

Tasar's black eyes twinkled. "Then hire them. I'm sure they can do what Darkstriders have been unable to do for over a decade. Think about all the wealth and power you will gain. Is 300,000 crowns really that much?"

Was it? Artis rubbed his chin. He could get what he gave Tasar back in additional taxes. Even after he recouped all his crowns, why not keep those taxes going? After all, he was doing it for the good of the people, of course. He nodded. "Okay, I'll do it." He looked over at Lena. "Go the Treasury and withdraw 150,000 crowns and give it to him."

Lena gulped. "What do I write down as the reason for the withdrawal?"

Tasar smiled at Artis. "Civic improvements."

After Artis nodded, Lena hurried out of the room.

Tasar reached his hand out. "Pleasure doing business with you."

"Don't fail me," Artis said.

"I never do."

GALIN, Jena, and Ellis followed Nyna into his office. As soon as they were inside, Nyna slammed the door shut. His veins were popping out of his forehead. "What the hell were you thinking?"

Jena backed away. "I'm sorry."

"Hey, relax, we were just having a little fun. Besides, we didn't even start it," Ellis said.

Nyna glared at Galin. "Do you know how much danger you put the school in for just being here?"

Galin swallowed. "I know. I'm sorry. I'll just walk away next time."

Nyna motioned them to sit down in the lumpy chairs along the wall. "Please, sit down." He sighed as he sat behind his maple desk. "Sumia wasn't wrong when she said you three would be a handful."

Galin's eyes lit up. "Have you seen her?"

Nyna nodded. "She checks on you quite frequently. It's pretty annoying, actually."

"How come she never stopped by?" Jena asked. "I want her to be here when we get married."

Galin's eyes sagged as he looked at Jena's smile.

"Maybe it's for the best," Nyna said. "She brought her father out of hiding and the Darkstriders know it." He glared at Galin. "That's why causing problems with Beldroth's daughter was foolish."

Galin nodded. He was so careful to stay in the background, although it was nearly impossible for him since he was the only human male child learning magic at the school. His saving grace was that Tadus School of Magic was considered neutral territory. The Wizards were very careful not to let any communications leave the island. The typical student left home to attend Tadus School of Magic and wasn't heard from again for at least six years. But, Galin wasn't typical and he knew it. Worse yet, everyone else knew it, too. "I'm sorry, and it won't happen again. I know the risk you're taking. I—"

Nyna glared at him. "No, you do not! We put the entire school in jeopardy by allowing you to attend. You're not some war mage or healer they'd have to fight later on. You're their prophesied enemy. The one who will destroy them. They've destroyed entire villages looking for you. People have died because of you! That's why you must do what I say without question." He stared right at Jena. "It's obvious you didn't do what I told you to do about *her*."

Jena blinked. "What? What are you talking about?"

"You aren't my father," Galin retorted. "All my life everyone told me what to do and almost none of them were right. I know the dangers and I'll deal with them as I see fit. I—"

Jena punched Galin in the arm. "What did he tell you?"

"I told him to put off your wedding for your own good," Nyna said. "Whenever anything happens to you, he starts to lose control, without fail. You see, dragons have natural protection against their own magic. That's why their little ones don't kill themselves by accident. You see, dragons are born this way, but Galin was not."

Jena's eyes welled up as if her hopes were shattered. "Are you?"

Galin shook his head. "It's something we're going to talk about, but it's a decision for us to make, not some ancient Snow Elf."

Ellis rolled his eyes. "Told you we should leave."

Nyna sighed. "Well, I guess you have your wish." He

fumbled through some papers on his desk. "I got this note today from the Headmaster. If I can find it…"

Was Galin being kicked out? His first act after no longer hiding his true name was about to end in failure. How could he reclaim the throne if he couldn't even pass magic school?

"Here it is," Nyna said as he pulled a crumpled piece of paper from the basket. He looked up at the confused Galin. "I got angry after I read it."

"What does it say?" Ellis asked.

Nyna pulled out a monocle and put it in his right eye. "You have one more chance the pass your final test and then you have to go, regardless of whether you pass or not. To come back and complete your training, you have to pass it."

"What if I don't leave?" Galin asked.

Nyna pulled the monocle out of his eye and tossed it on the desk. "The faculty will turn you over to the Darkstriders."

Galin jumped up. "You can't do that! The school is neutral. That's why Sumia sent me here."

Nyna nodded. "I know, that's why I was so mad after reading this."

"When is it?" Galin asked.

"Tomorrow morning," Nyna replied.

Ellis rolled his eyes. "Are you trying to make him fail? If that's what you're doing, just let us leave now."

Galin rose to his feet. "I will pass your test and start my mission. Let's get out of here." He led Jena and Ellis out of Nyna's office. *How am I going to pass that stupid test?*

CHAPTER 3

Finals

Galin, Ellis, and Jena were walking down the stone hallway towards an elaborate wooden door. His chest got tighter with each step. "I hope I don't screw this up."

Jena held his hand. "I believe in you."

Galin looked right into her eyes. "I believe in us." He leaned closer to Jena.

Ellis pushed them apart. "You two are just plain sick." He pushed Galin towards the door. "Go take your damned test so we can get out of here."

As Galin touched the door, it opened. Nyna was standing in the doorway. "Come in, Galin."

Jena and Ellis started to follow him.

Nyna held up his hand. "No, not this time."

Jena frowned. "Why? We've been with him for every other test."

"I want him to pass," Nyna whispered. "His best chance is for you two to keep away."

Jena gave Galin a hug. "I love you. Good luck. I'll be waiting for you to come back."

Galin looked at Nyna.

He rolled his eyes. "I'll make sure they're present when you're done. Now come on."

Galin followed Nyna into the dark room. As they entered, the door slammed shut. Crystals on the walls lit up, illuminating the whole room. Unlike the rest of the school, the walls were completely bare. In the center was a stone circle with a glowing sphere suspended above it. "I'm ready."

Nyna nodded. "This is a combat test. To put it simply, a rescue mission. A gnome necromancer has captured a boy from the local village. He needs the boy's liver as a spell component to create a ghoul. You have to stop him."

Galin tapped his sword at his side. "I'm ready."

"One more thing," Nyna said. "Unlike the other tests, I am not permitted to stop this test at any time. If you die in this test, you die in real life."

Galin gulped.

"Do you understand?" Nyna's eyes softened. "Focus your defensive magical skills. When you feel like you are losing control, think about you and Jena on the throne in Staerdale Castle after you free the world." He put his hand on Galin's shoulder. "I know you can do this. Now, go and save that little boy."

Galin shook Nyna's hand. "Thanks for everything you have done."

Nyna nodded.

Galin stepped inside the glowing sphere. The plain stone walls and Nyna were consumed by the blinding light. It was so bright that Galin slammed his eyes shut.

After a moment, the warmth of the Tadus School of Magic was replaced by a cold wind. He opened his eyes. The moon was full and the trees were covered with a layer of fluffy, white snow. Unlike his other tests, this one seemed real.

In front of him was a small tower in the middle of a pasture, with houses along the base of the tower like goslings following their mother. Was the necromancer the ruler of the tower? Were there humans in the town? Probably not. Galin grunted. The only gnomes he'd ever known were the ones he met in school. They generally kept to themselves. Why should they be any different? The tower had to be it, right? A cold breeze stung his cheeks. Galin trudged through the snow towards the tower. He didn't have much time.

As he walked through the tiny village surrounding the tower, there were no lights inside the houses; even the tavern was closed. Galin smiled. Maybe they didn't put that much detail into their test. Or maybe it was that late at night. Quietly, he moved through the gnome village unnoticed.

The base of the tower was unremarkable. The stone walls glistened in the moonlight. Keeping his distance, Galin crept around the tower. A small wooden door with two bushes on either side came into view. *Here we go,* Galin thought. Somewhere inside was a little boy about to be murdered. He had to be careful, but quick. As he approached the door, Galin noticed a light coming from a third-story window. Maybe he was up there. Was it too late? He looked around. No guards, nothing at all. A trusting mage? He opened the door and went inside.

The light flickered on the floor from the candle in the sconce. Galin drew his sword. His leather boots were silent on the rough wooden floor. The entranceway opened up into a large circular room with tapestries decorating its walls. On the far side of the room was a staircase going up. His head moved like it was on a swivel as he searched the room. Besides a fireplace for cooking and a simple table with four chairs, the room was empty. Galin blinked. Four chairs? Why four chairs? If someone was in solitude, why would he or she have four chairs at the dinner table? His hands tightened on the hilt. There must be more than one.

A boy's scream echoed down the stairs.

Galin's head jerked towards the stairs. *Am I too late?* He had to pass the test. Was he too cautious? No time. He bolted up the stairs. Galin burst onto the second floor. It was another single room. Bookcases lined the walls. In the center of the room was a table that an alchemist would use. *I thought he was a necromancer?* Galin took another look around. Nothing. He continued up the stairs, not a reckless sprint, but a deliberate ascension.

When Galin reached the top, he pressed against the wall.

"Hold the wretched thing still," a raspy voice said. "If you mess it up, I'll use *your* liver. Got it, Zilben?"

"Please, please stop!" cried the boy's voice.

Galin blinked as he heard the gnomes slap the boy, hard.

"Master Xogrim, please, I'm trying," the younger voice said.

There were at least two of them. Galin could take one out fast, but the other would kill him. What did Nyna say? What was the key to this test? Defense. Just like Nyna taught him, he willed his anger to grow using images of how that boy would be forever cursed if he failed him. Tiny electrical arcs, like lightning from the sky, jumped across his skin. His eyes began to glow. Control…he had to maintain control like Nyna and his adoptive father, Brock Feran, had taught him.

"Finally, you got the kid tied down, Zilben. Now pass me the knife," Xogrim said.

Now or never. Galin charged into the room with his skin and sword glowing.

"What's that?" Zilben asked. He was a short gnome with dark hair wearing a black robe.

Xogrim's face was as red as his robes. "Get him, now!"

Galin charged at Zilben. As soon as his sword touched his robe, the robe ignited. The screaming gnome ran down the stairs.

Xogrim had his wand out, mumbling a few inaudible words. Three fiery objects appeared in front of the wand.

Galin faced Xogrim. *Think defense.* The glow on his

skin became more intense, brighter. With his sword raised, he charged at Xogrim.

The fiery bolts flew through the air at Galin. As they hit his glowing skin, they vanished, as if absorbed by the dragon magic.

Xogrim used the wand again and the fiery bolts vanished, just like before.

Galin's glowing sword slammed into the gnome's head, severing it from his body. He looked over at the stairs. No sign of the apprentice coming back. He closed his eyes as he forced images of his wedding to Jena. The tingling receded. His skin, sword, and eyes no longer glowed. It was over. Galin walked over to the table. The shirtless, blond-haired boy was tied to the table. "Let me get you out of this."

After Galin had untied him, the boy sat up and hugged him. "Thank you. He was going to kill me!"

"It's okay, I've got you," Galin said as he embraced the child. The room flashed, hurting his eyes.

"Well done," Nyna said. His smiled stretched from ear to ear. "Very well done."

Galin blinked. He was back at the school. "Thank you."

Nyna motioned Galin to the door. "Let's get you back to your friends. You've got a graduation to attend."

"When?"

"Late this afternoon. Jena and Ellis are already packing their things. It was the headmaster's orders," Nyna said. "I'm sorry."

Galin smiled. "Thank you for everything."

Nyna shook his head. "No, you need to thank Sumia. Let's go."

Galin followed Nyna out of the Test Chamber.

Hours later, Galin, Jena, and Ellis were waiting outside the headmaster's office with their belongings. They were sitting on the bench along the marble walls that were normally occupied by misbehaving students, but today was different. Normally, graduations were held in the courtyard, with fanfare and family. Galin was a special case and he knew it.

Nyna and a Dark Elf were walking down the hall towards Galin and his friends. "Are we late?" Nyna asked.

Galin held his breath as the Dark Elf approached. This was not a young student or even one of the instructors. His sunken, black eyes twinkled at him. "Sir, I don't know your friend."

Nyna cleared his throat. "Oh, forgive me. This is Daylor. We've been friends for at least 120 years."

The Dark Elf with salt-and-pepper shoulder-length hair smiled. "More like 150."

Nyna rubbed his chin. "Could be. Let's see if he's ready for us." He knocked on the door.

"Come in," a voice said from behind the door.

Galin, Jena, Ellis, and Daylor followed Nyna into the headmaster's office.

A fair-skinned Vulwin Elf sat behind a cedar desk with an elaborate border carved into it. He wore red robes with a scarlet hood and gold trim. The walls were lined with overfilled bookcases. "Is this he?" Zelphar asked.

"Yes, Headmaster," Nyna said. He pushed Galin right in front of Zelphar's desk. "He's a very gifted student and one that will need to return someday."

Zelphar glared at Nyna. "Why?"

Nyna sighed. "I've taught him everything I know about dragon magic, but I am not a master. We need to find one for him."

"It's not safe to keep him here, Nyna, you know that." Zelphar smiled at Galin. "Young man, you have done better in that last test than many others with far more years of training." He pulled out a rolled-up scroll and gave it to Galin. "Here's your diploma, congratulations. Now, leave my school."

Nyna's face reddened.

Daylor was stone-faced.

Galin blinked. "That's it? Great job, now get out?"

Ellis glared at Zelphar. "You're a goblin's ass."

Zelphar shook his head. "It's just too dangerous. The Darkstriders have already threatened us about letting them into our school for periodic inspections. What would happen if they found *him* here?" he asked, pointing directly at Galin. "They'd shut down the school and kill all of us."

"They would never get onto the island and you damn well know it," Nyna retorted.

Zelphar jumped to his feet. "One more crack out of you and you'll go with them."

"At least I wouldn't be in the company of a coward."

"Stop it!" Galin yelled. "When I first came here, I was told that the school was neutral and not to worry about the others who attend school here." His burning eyes bore into Zelphar. "Obviously, that's not true. Why don't you fight? Did you even help when they took over the kingdom? Or were you 'neutral' then, too? I'm not neutral, and I will give them a reason to fear me. If they defeat us, guess where they're coming next? Will the Darkstriders treat you like they did the other Vulwin Elves? Of course they will. I am just a higher priority than *you*!" That familiar tingle ran through his body. His skin began to glow.

Zelphar leaped back, knocking his chair to the floor.

Nyna put his hand on Galin's shoulder. "Settle down."

Galin ripped out of Nyna's grasp. "Why?"

"Control."

Galin glared at Nyna. He was right and he knew it. "Okay." He closed his eyes and his power receded.

Zelphar pointed at Galin. "You see, he's dangerous. Get him out of here!"

Daylor smiled at Zelphar. "He's right, you are a coward. If you don't let the boy come back when there is a master of Dragon Magic available, I'll give you to the Darkstriders myself. How loud can you scream?"

Nyna motioned everyone out of Zelphar's office. "Let's go."

Back in the hall, Nyna smiled at Galin. "Your adoptive father is waiting for you at Vebaco in the Lazy Spoon. I already contacted him."

"Thank you," Galin said.

"It was my pleasure." Nyna took a rough diamond from his spell component pouch on his belt. "Dit onska ni jeg. Dit onska ni jeg. Dit onska ni jeg." A dark circle appeared on the wall.

"Bexon's Dimensional Tunnel?" Jena asked as she grabbed her bag.

"Of course," Nyna replied. "It'll take you to Vebaco."

Ellis tossed his bag over his shoulder. "I'm gone." He stepped into the tunnel.

"Good-bye," Jena said as she entered the portal.

Galin put his sword on his hip and slung his pack on his back. "I'll never forget what you taught me." He extended his hand to Nyna.

"You will always have at least one ally here," Nyna said as he shook his hand. "Now go and raise your army to free us all."

"I will." Galin stepped into the tunnel and disappeared.

LATER, Nyna was sitting behind his desk and Daylor was sitting across from him, sipping tea. "I'm going to do it," Nyna said.

"Do what?" Daylor asked.

Nyna rubbed his eyes. "I'm tired of being neutral. Why can't I choose a side, like you did?"

"You can." Daylor leaned forward. "If he is the one, why wouldn't we rid the land of the Darkstriders? We could augment his army with an army of war mages, seers, and necromancers. Think about it. They wouldn't stand a chance."

Nyna pulled out a scroll and began to write.

"What are you doing?" Daylor asked.

"I'm writing a letter to the Shadow Mage."

Daylor raised an eyebrow. "He'll help?"

Nyna looked up. "Can you think of a better staging area to attack them? The Tower of the Shadow Mage is due south of Staerdale Castle."

Daylor nodded. "And he's got an army of his own. That's why Tanyl did the truce with him rather than fight him. It's rumored that he controls a dragon." He headed for the door. "I've got to get back. They'll be missing me at Staerdale Castle by now."

"Why? Just stay with me," Nyna said.

"How can I spy on them if I'm here? There are advantages to being on Tanyl's council." Daylor grinned. "After all, I'm a Dark Elf; deception comes naturally to me."

Nyna nodded. "I guess you're right." He continued writing his letter to the Shadow Mage.

CHAPTER 4

Vebaco

Galin appeared just inside the wood line outside the tiny village of Vebaco. The warm, summer breeze blew through Galin's brown hair. His blue eyes twinkled when he spotted Jena. "Everyone okay?"

Ellis nodded his head. "Yeah. I wish I could do that. I could go anywhere and do anything."

Jena giggled. "Think of all the crowns you could steal."

"Yes, exactly," Ellis said, pointing at Jena.

Galin frowned. "You're not that much of a thief and you know it."

Ellis grinned. "We all have our faults."

"Let's go," Galin said. "Father is waiting for us." He stepped off through the field towards the village.

As they entered the village of Vebaco, good memories of their hometown of Crey Village flashed through Galin's mind. He couldn't help but smile. The market square was littered with booths and vendors selling their wares from their carts. The smell of baking bread invaded his nostrils.

"Where are we going again?" Jena asked.

"The Lazy Spoon," Galin said. "They're supposed to meet us there."

Along the edges of the market square were no more than seven simple and unkempt buildings. "Over there," Ellis said as he pointed to the only three-story building in town. "Looks like it's an inn, too."

Galin bit his lip. "Damn."

"What?" Jena asked.

"We've got no money. Hopefully, Father has enough," Galin said.

Ellis giggled. "We don't need our *own* money."

Galin frowned. "You promised to stop stealing."

Ellis crossed his fingers behind his back. "I know I did. I'll only do it as a last resort, okay?"

"I guess. Come on." Galin headed inside the Lazy Spoon.

Even though the outside was rundown and not maintained, the inside was beautiful. The bar along the left wall was made out of a polished mahogany. All the stools surrounding it were occupied by poorly dressed patrons. On the far wall was a raised stage with a man sitting on a stool playing a lute. Its sweet melody brought a smile to Galin's face. Tables and benches filled with humans were sprinkled throughout the large room. "Let's look for Father," Galin said to Jena.

Ellis pointed at the bar. "I'll get us a room and some ale."

"With what money?" Jena asked.

Ellis laughed. "This is an emergency. Trust me." He disappeared into the crowd.

"Someday, he'll get us into trouble. Come on." Galin waded into the sea of people with his eyes bouncing from face to face, looking for the last member of his family that was still alive.

Jena tugged at Galin's arm. "There's Mother!" She raced across the room to a couple sitting at a large, round table with three empty seats. Keya's brown eyes complemented her shoulder-length, blond hair. She wore a cream-colored robe, typical for an elder priestess of Odella. The large man had his brown hair pulled back into a ponytail. He was wearing a plain tan tunic with a long sword by his side. Both were slamming back the local ale.

Galin slowly sat down across from his father. He reached across the table towards Brock Feran. "I missed you. They wouldn't let me out to see you."

Brock took a swig. "It's okay, sire."

Galin glared at him. "Are you sure you should be calling me that here?"

"But yoooou are the prophesied king," Brock said. He blinked. "We're heeere to raise an army, remember?"

Jena looked at Keya. "Is he drunk?"

Keya's glossy eyes twinkled. "A little. We've been waiting for you for a bit now."

Brock nodded. "Yeah, Nyyyna said yooou would be here long—*hiccup*—ago. We've got a room, but you'll need to get one."

"Do you have any money?" Galin asked.

Keya smiled. "Sumia gave us plenty to get started. This town is a perfect place to begin. There are no Darkstriders here and no one likes them, either."

Galin glanced over at Jena. "I feel stupider listening to them."

Jena beamed at her mother. "I would like to get a few things from the house. When are we going back?"

Keya frowned and said nothing.

"What is it?" Jena asked.

Brock sipped his ale. "Soon after you left, the Darkstriders came and killed everyone. The Vulwin Elves tried to help, but they were overwhelmed by the Feral Orc legions."

Tears flowed down Keya's cheeks. "Not just the people; they burned everything to the ground. It's almost like Crey Village never existed. All those people were killed, without even knowing why."

Galin looked down at the table. "It's my fault. It's all my fault. My friends, all gone."

"I'm still here, you orc's ass," Ellis said as he put three ales down on the table. "I got us two rooms."

"Two rooms?" Jena asked.

Ellis smirked. "You two cramp my style." He slid into the chair. "What are we…they're loaded!" Ellis laughed.

"Don't you care that your father is dead?" Galin

demanded. "I know that you hated the bakery, but you must have loved him."

"Of course I loved him," Ellis snapped. "But I don't know that he's dead. For all I know, he may not have been in the village when they attacked. I just don't know. Until I know for sure, there is a chance he is still alive and I'm going with that."

Jena smiled. "For once, he's got a point."

Ellis clapped his hands together. "So, are we getting drunk or something? Like father, like son?"

Galin frowned. "No. Let's just call it a night."

"That's fine with me," Jena said as she stood up.

"Nooo, we can't wait. We haave to start recruuiting now," Brock said as he nearly spilled his ale on the table.

"We'll do that in the morning," Galin said.

Brock shook his head. "No, we've waited long enough." He climbed on top of the round table.

"What is he doing?" Jena asked.

Galin turned away in disgust. "No idea."

Ellis chuckled. "This is great."

"Hey, sit down!" the bartender yelled from across the room.

Brock held up his hand. "Just a minute. I've got an announcement." He cleared his throat. "People of Vebaaco, I have got good news. Prince Galin V of the Ravenward is alive and well!"

"Who?" a beer wench asked.

"The rightful heir to the throne, before that bastard Kade betrayed us all," an older man said. "So, what?"

Galin swallowed. This was not how he wanted to recruit people, but could he stop his father now? Brock had patiently waited for over a year to finish his mission that he'd promised to the only female knight in the kingdom of Axain before she sacrificed herself to save them all. He looked over at Jena with a questioning glance.

Jena nodded. "It's time."

"Where is he?" another yelled. "Is he as drunk as you?"

Laughter erupted.

Brock's face reddened. "He's right here," he said, pointing at Galin.

This was it. The first step to avenge his family and overthrow the Darkstriders and Kade the Usurper. Galin stood up. "I am Galin V of Ravenward. I am raising an army to retake the kingdom."

The room burst into laughter.

"Sit down!" a man yelled.

"Shut up!" the older man said. "Hear him out!"

Galin cleared his throat. Was that a supporter? "We are just now starting to form our army. I am looking for volunteers to help us free our lands. If you join us and you survive, your loyalty to the kingdom will be rewarded. If not, the bards will sing of your heroics throughout history. This is the time to choose. Do you want to be slaves to the whims of the Darkstriders or do you want your freedom?"

A red-haired man in his twenties stood up. "If by some miracle you do become king, how do we know you will be any different than they are? We don't know you."

Galin blinked. How indeed? They didn't know him, nor did he know them. Heck, he'd never heard of this town until Nyna sent him here. He grinned. "Because they fear me. They believe that I am the prophesied king who will destroy them. Once they are gone, I will create a government for all of us, not just the nobility. If you come with us now, you could become a noble yourself."

Brock stepped back, unbalancing the table. It flipped over and he crashed to the floor.

Everyone laughed.

Keya rushed to his side.

The bartender came from behind the bar, approaching Galin. "Even if we wanted to help you, we can't."

"Why not?" Ellis asked. "Are you a coward?"

"No, the mayor has the local militia on alert every night," the bartender said. "If you want us to help you, you've got to talk to him."

Galin extended his hand. "Galin."

"I'm Paul," the bartender said. "His house is just outside the center of town."

"Why are you always on alert?" Galin asked.

Paul clamped his lips shut. "Talk to the mayor. If he agrees, I'll go with you, and I'm sure there'll be others." He pointed down at Brock. "Take care of your friend before he ends up in the stocks."

Galin looked at his adoptive father. "Let's go." Galin and Ellis hoisted Brock to his feet and brought him to his room.

~

THE NEXT MORNING, Galin led the small band down the dusty road out of the market square. Thankfully, Brock and Keya brought their horses for them, since they didn't have them when he was in school. Galin's mount was a brown and white painted mare named after the female knight who saved his life when he was a baby, Thea. The horse had grown a little over the past year, but not much.

Jena urged Tyra, her brown mare with a white patch over her left eye, to move up next to Galin. "What are we going to say? I mean, what if he turns us in?"

Ellis shrugged. "Then he turns us in." His short, tan mare, which was full of black spots and a black mane, neighed. He grinned. "See, even Runt agrees with me. Stop worrying already."

Just ahead was a simple, small log cabin-style home with smoke coming out of the chimney. Galin looked back at Brock and Keya. "Are you two ready?"

Brock nodded. "Yeah, I'm ready, sire." He grinned at Keya. "I'll never get used to calling him that," he whispered.

She leaned close to him. "Me either. He'll always be little Seth to me."

Galin dismounted Thea in front of the mayor's home. He tied Thea off onto a crude hitching post.

Jena and the rest did the same. She motioned him to the door. "After you."

Galin grunted. "All right, let's see what he wants." As he approached the door, it flew open.

A balding, middle-aged man wearing a brown shirt and red pajama pants beamed at them. "Galin, right?"

Galin nodded.

"I'm Amet Rowcroft, the village mayor. Paul told me you were coming." He waved them through. "Please, come in." They followed Amet inside.

The pleasant smell of bacon being cooked over an open fire reminded Galin that he didn't have breakfast that morning. The mayor's home was simple and modest. Amet sat down in an over-sized cushion chair and motioned the others to sit on the couch across from him. Galin looked over at the fireplace. An older, yet still attractive, woman was fixing breakfast. "Is that your wife?"

Amet nodded. "Yes, I'm sorry." He stood up. "Honey, this is Prince Galin V of Ravenward. Sire, this is my wife, Sarah."

She curtsied. "My lord."

Galin swallowed. Was it right that they treat him like that? He hadn't done anything, yet. Well, unless you count putting them in danger. He held up his hand. "Please don't, just Galin."

"As you wish," Amet said as he sat back down. "Well, Galin, how can I help you?"

Galin leaned back into the couch. "I'm starting to raise an army to take back my kingdom."

Amet smiled. "That's a nice thought. But, really? Come on, you're just a boy."

He glared at Amet. "I will take it back and avenge my parents." Galin looked over at Brock. "And Sally."

Brock smiled.

Amet sighed. "We can't get involved. We are just a small farming village; well, used to be."

Jena leaned forward. "What happened?"

"Well, when King Galin IV ruled, we were protected from…creatures that attacked our livestock. At that time, we were one of the biggest suppliers of beef and chicken to Staerdale Castle. Heck, we used to supply the Vulwin Elves, too, even after they put that tax on going through Port Eldham," Amet said. "But, since the Darkstriders took over, we have to fend for ourselves. You see, Dark Elves don't like beef that much. At the same time, we are no threat to them, so they leave us alone."

Galin nodded. "For now. What you don't know is that they've been hunting for me for the past fifteen years. Once they get me, what do you think they'll do then?"

Amet grunted. "But if we openly support you, they'll kill all of us, or worse."

"We aren't asking for open support," Brock said. "That would be foolish. What we want is to take some volunteers from your village to help us."

"What's your plan?" Amet asked.

Brock smiled. "To build up some forces and—"

Amet pointed to Galin. "I want to hear it from him."

Galin gulped. He hadn't thought that far ahead, yet. Heck, he wasn't even ready to start recruiting. But once Brock opened his mouth, how could he say no? "There are a lot of former knights and warriors in hiding, many of which have been waiting for my return."

"What does that have to do with my people?" Amet asked.

Brock crossed his arms. "We need a place to recruit and train our army to go against the Darkstriders. But, we have to secure it first."

Amet jumped to his feet. "You will not do that here. They would definitely come and kill everyone in the village. Out of the question."

Galin shook his head. "You don't understand, we need to go east, close to the Wailing Mountains. We are just asking for some of your warriors, that's all."

Sarah glared at Amet. "You're always complaining about them and now when you have a chance to do something, you find every reason not to help?" She threw his breakfast into the fire in disgust as she bolted into the other room.

Amet sighed. "She's right. I'll help you."

"Thank you," Galin said.

"On one condition; you need to take care of those creatures attacking our livestock. I've had to keep the village militia on alert ever since they started attacking the livestock. Each night, they get closer to the village. I fear they'll eventually attack us." Amet shifted in his seat. "All we know is that they seem to come from the Infernal Grotto, deep inside the Misty Forest."

"What creatures?" Ellis asked.

"Zombies." Amet sank into his chair. "The walking dead."

Galin nodded. "Okay, if we rid you of that problem,

you'll give us some of your militia?" He felt the mortified stares from everyone in the room. Galin extended his hand to Amet.

"Deal." Amet shook Galin's hand. "Just one more thing; you aren't the first party that went there to stop them. We don't know what happened to them, we can only assume the worst." His eyes became puffy. "Please be careful."

"We will." Galin led the group back outside.

After they mounted up, Ellis frowned. "How do we fight zombies?"

Galin couldn't even look at him. "I've got no idea." *What have I gotten us into?*

CHAPTER 5

Tasar on the Hunt

asar's red robes with purple trim blew in the early evening breeze as he entered Vebaco. The tiny village had only one tavern, which was also the inn. Even for a tiny village, the pub was lively. He pushed through the door. As the Dark Elf entered the tavern, no one spoke. Silence, utter silence fell upon the once lively crowd. His thin lips curled. "Relax, I'm not a Darkstrider. I'm just here for a drink." As he moved over towards the bar, the stools suddenly became empty.

Paul slapped on a plastic smile. "What can I get you?"

Tasar tossed five crowns on the bar. "Whiskey and a little...conversation."

Paul frowned. "I'm a quiet guy myself," he said as he poured some whiskey in a glass.

"That's too bad. How about I talk and you just listen?" Tasar asked. He put on a gold ring with elven script engraved along the band. There was an emerald with a diamond in the center mounted on the face of the ring. He tapped it and smiled.

"I can do that," Paul said.

Tasar slammed back his whiskey. "I was in Grug looking for a friend of mine, Brock Feran."

Paul swallowed as he looked away. He pulled a damp cloth from behind the bar and started to wipe it down. "Never heard of him."

Tasar motioned for more whiskey. "Too bad."

Paul refilled the glass. "Sorry."

"Ever been to Grug?" Tasar asked.

Paul rubbed his chin. "Yeah, that's the port south of Methos Lake, right?"

Tasar nodded. "Yes." He began to rub his ring. The diamond within the emerald began to glow. "I met a jeweler who knew him. Apparently, he purchased a necklace for his new lover. Everyone has to move on, I suppose."

"Why do you say that?" Paul asked.

Tasar feigned surprised. "Well, his wife was killed by the Darkstriders. It was done in such a brutal way that he went crazy." His ring glowed brightly. "He went crazy. I can understand it; can't you?"

Paul blinked, as if his own will vanished in the glow of Tasar's ring. "I can understand it. More whiskey?"

"Thank you." Tasar pushed his glass towards Paul. "He made outlandish claims about overthrowing the Darkstriders." Tasar began to laugh. "He even claims that the feared prophesied king was with him." He shook his head as he sipped his whiskey. The ring was glowing a bright green with a white center. "Are you sure he hasn't come here? The merchant was certain he was on his way here—to Vebaco, I mean."

"What does he look like?" Paul asked.

"He's a strong human in his thirties. He used to be a blacksmith until his wife died. He's traveling with a woman about the same age. Her name is Keya. She's a priestess of Odella." Tasar rubbed his ring, making it glow even more. "Are you sure you didn't see them?"

Sweat formed on Paul's forehead. "I...yes, they were here yesterday. They were asking for volunteers to go with them."

Tasar smiled. "Good."

"But, they weren't alone," Paul said.

Tasar raised an eyebrow. "Really?"

"Yes, there were two boys and a girl with them. They were around 16 years old or something. Brock was too drunk to recruit anyone, but the boy spoke like a king," Paul said. "They wanted us to go with them to take on the Darkstriders."

"Did anyone go?" Tasar asked.

Paul shook his head. "No, everyone's in the militia here. We have to protect our livestock from the undead."

Tasar blinked. "Undead?"

Paul nodded. "They made a deal with the mayor that if they stopped the undead problem, he'd send some of the militia to join their cause."

"Did they accept?"

"Yeah, they left yesterday."

Tasar snapped his fingers and his ring stopped glowing. He stared at Paul's blank face. "Thanks for the whiskey."

Paul rubbed his eyes. "Sure, sure thing. I…I've got to…do something." He moved towards the other end of the bar.

Tasar grinned. The Ring of Praflyn never failed him, especially when used against the weak-minded humans. He sipped his whiskey. If Galin was going after a necromancer, he'd already put himself in danger. He'd probably lose, but if he was the prophesied king, he may just survive; unless he tipped the odds in the necromancer's favor. Tasar tossed a few more crowns on the bar and left the Lazy Spoon.

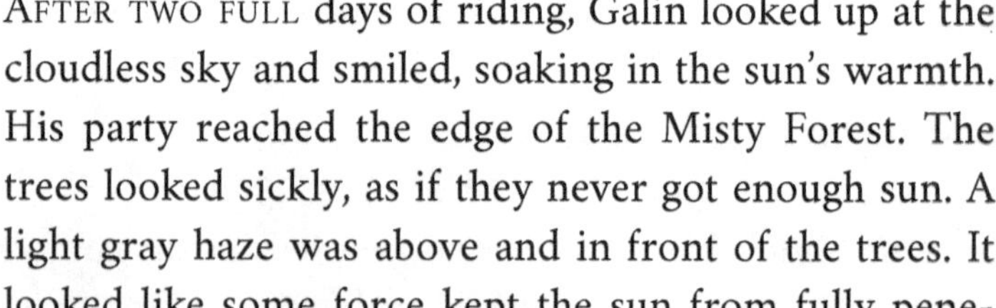

AFTER TWO FULL days of riding, Galin looked up at the cloudless sky and smiled, soaking in the sun's warmth. His party reached the edge of the Misty Forest. The trees looked sickly, as if they never got enough sun. A light gray haze was above and in front of the trees. It looked like some force kept the sun from fully penetrating the fog-like haze. Galin grinned at Ellis.

"That just looks creepy," Ellis said, pointing at the Misty Forest ahead.

Galin grinned. "Scared?"

Jena giggled.

Ellis shook his head. "Of course not, I...I was thinking of Jena, that's all."

Keya laughed.

Brock grinned. "Then why don't you lead us in?"

"Um...Galin should, after all he's the prince," Ellis replied.

Galin patted Thea on the head. "Come on, girl, let's show him how it's done." He urged her forward into the mist. The warm afternoon sun seemed to disappear when his skin touched the mist. It was cold and damp. The further they went inside, the darker it became. Galin's head moved like a swivel with his eyes trying to see behind every tree and bush.

Jena rubbed her upper arms. "I don't like it here. Maybe Ellis was right."

Runt neighed.

"Runt agrees with her," Ellis said. "Let's get out of here. We don't need those guys. We can always find more without doing crazy stuff."

Galin stopped Thea and stared right at Ellis. "No, I gave my word that we would help those people."

"How are we supposed to stop those creatures?" Ellis asked. "We don't even know what they are, or even where they are. Are we supposed to just wander around the woods until we run across one of them?"

Brock's face fell. "Sire, he's got a point."

Ellis was emboldened. "How do we defeat them? If they couldn't do it swords, what are we supposed to do?"

Galin's face reddened. "Then go, see if I care."

Keya held up her hands. "Stop it, all of you!" she yelled. "It's the mist doing this to you. The mist is amplifying your fears."

Galin nodded. "Okay. I'm sorry."

Ellis sighed. "Me too. But, you're still an orc's ass."

Galin, with Jena by his side, led them deep into the Misty Forest for another few hours. The sun began to sink over the horizon.

"Damn it," Ellis said. "I don't want to be here in the dark."

"If it gets too dark, I'll just cast Odella's Light, like I did at Porp Hollows," Jena said.

"Those things should be heading towards the livestock soon," Brock said. "We need to listen for them. We may get an idea where they're coming from."

Keya nodded. "Assuming that they stay together."

"Do we have any reason to think they don't?" Galin asked. "If they only come out at night, you'd assume there would be limited places for them to hide during the day."

Ellis laughed. "What are you expecting? A vampire or something? Those aren't real."

Keya shook her head. "No, Ellis, the undead are very real."

Galin dismounted. "Let's stop here for a bit."

"I'll start the fire," Ellis said as he jumped off Runt.

"No fire," Brock said. "We're not camping, we're listening for them. We can't see well in the dark, but we can hear good enough."

Galin nodded. "Jena, have your light spell ready. We'll need it once we hear something."

Keya began to rummage through her spell components bag. "I've got a spell that can help us, if they are undead."

Ellis rolled his eyes. "It's probably a pack of wolves or something. You're all crazy." He slumped down next to a tree.

They were silent. The minutes seemed liked hours, and those two hours seemed like days. Every time a leaf rustled or the wind blew, Galin closed his eyes to listen more intently. Creatures, with either two or four legs, would make that distinct sound of walking through the forest on ground covered with dry leaves.

Crunch. Crunch. Crunch.

Galin's eyes flew open. Something walking? It had to be. He tapped Jena, who was already alert.

Crunch. Crunch. Crunch.

Where are they going? Galin thought. He closed his eyes again, focusing on the sounds.

Crunch. Crunch. Crunch.

Closer, they were coming to closer. Just passing near them or— "Jena, the light, now!"

Jena whipped out a piece of milky quartz. "Wen opel gia. Wen opel gia. Wen opel gia!" A bright light came from the crystal.

Everything within twenty-five yards suddenly became visible, and Galin almost wished it hadn't.

Jena screamed.

There were at least ten of them. They had no hair and their skin was rotting off. Their eyes were...missing. Galin blinked. Why would *these things* attack livestock? "To arms!" He jumped up with his sword drawn.

Brock joined his adopted son.

Ellis stood up, facing the opposite direction. "Hey, Galin, there's some behind us, too."

Keya looked up at Jena. "You know what to do?"

Jena shook her head.

Her mother frowned. "Watch me." She looked up at Galin. "Don't let the liches touch you. They are immune to non-magical weapons."

Brock frowned. "How do we fight them?"

Keya shook her head. "Just let me know when they are all within 20 yards."

Galin nodded. "Okay." Would dragon magic work? Would his sword be non-magical if he used his powers?

Keya knelt down, pulling out a silver Symbol of Odella. It was an eye with three stars converging into the center being carried by a dove. She bowed her head in prayer.

Ellis backed into Galin as the liches came closer. "How about now?"

"Not yet!" Galin yelled. His stomach wrenched. What was Keya doing? What if it didn't work? Did he even have a plan B? "Almost."

A lich swung its clawed hand at Brock, but he knocked it away with his sword. "That one's pretty damn close."

"Now!" Galin screamed.

Keya looked up to the sky, holding the Symbol of Odella above her head. "Gabort vandide, gabort ne. Jep se gabort."

A bright flash flew from the symbol. The liches within ten yards of her vanished into piles of ash. The others turned and lumbered away in fear. Keya collapsed to the ground.

"Keya!" Brock said as he rushed to her side. He picked up her head, holding it against his chest. A new strand of gray hair appeared among her bangs. "What happened?"

Keya's eyes opened. "They gone?"

Brock nodded. "What happened to you?" He helped Keya to her feet.

"When you cast that spell, you age four years," Keya said.

Jena blinked. "Can it be reversed by a prayer? Like the healing spells?"

Keya shook her head. "No, not this one."

Galin frowned. "I'm sorry about that."

"Well, hopefully you won't have to cast it too many more times," Ellis said. "You're pretty handy to have around."

Brock glared at Ellis.

Keya shook her head. "Even if I wanted to, I couldn't."

"Why not?" Galin asked.

"That can only be cast once every moon cycle," Keya replied. "Oh, the undead not disintegrated are sent home. If we follow them, we'll find the one who summoned them."

Galin nodded. "Okay."

Ellis grabbed Galin's shoulder. "Hey, stop. What are

we going to do when we find them? Our weapons won't work on them."

Galin wrenched himself out of Ellis' grasp. "We've got this, now come on. Have faith." *What are they going to do?* He led his small party after the wailing, lumbering liches.

CHAPTER 6

Infernal Grotto

Galin walked next to Jena, who was holding a brightly illuminated crystal from her Odella Light spell. His sword was drawn as they followed the hulking liches back towards their lair. Something was different; there was a soft, white glow around them. "What happens when they get back?" Galin asked as he looked back at Keya.

Keya was walking next to Brock and Ellis; both had their weapons drawn. "They will go into hibernation until the next moonrise."

Ellis blinked. "Really? Come on."

Keya nodded. "Yes." The sweat forming on her forehead glistened in the moonlight. "Let's just hope there aren't any more of them.

"How do we defeat those things?" Brock asked Keya.

"If we kill the one who summoned them, those souls will return to Odella's or Methos' realms and be at peace," Keya said.

Jena looked back at Keya. "Mother, are they basically slaves to the mage that summoned them?"

"Yes."

Galin nodded. "Then we know what we have to do." The mage who summoned those creatures must be elven or a human female or a gnome, just like at Tadus School of Magic. His powers protected him against offensive spells, but would it protect him against the undead? Would he be able to protect Jena?

Jena pointed at the liches, just inside the light emanating from her crystal. "They seem to be converging."

Galin pushed through the thorny underbrush. On the other side was a large mound. It was twice as tall as it was wide and crowned with thistles and dead trees. "They must have gone around the other side."

Ellis shook his head. "No way. Galin, this is too weird."

"Shut up," Jena said as she followed Galin.

Galin veered right at the base of the mound. His heart pounded with each step. Moans could be heard from the other side, not like the liches, but…something else. The leaves crunched underfoot as they moved around the mound. Light, there was light around the corner.

Jena doused her crystal and drew her short sword.

Galin gripped his sword tighter, trying to keep his hands from shaking. He put his hand up, stopping the group. Galin closed his eyes and listened. Moaning, all he heard was moaning. Whatever it was, it wasn't elven or human or gnome. He moved silently through the brush, just like his adoptive father taught him. The closer he got to the light, the more he hugged the trees. After all, he was trying to see what was ahead of them, not confront it.

"What's this?" a high, raspy male voice said. "Why are my liches back?"

Galin froze. That voice—no, that type of voice he'd heard before. He crept behind a large oak tree. He peered around its trunk and the entrance to the mound was in full view. There were two torches on either side of the entrance. The entrance was a cave mouth with more torchlight inside the cave. The black-robed gnome was no more than four feet tall. His skin was wrinkled, but his eyes were young. It was as if he'd aged by magical means; after all, every magical spell has a cost to the caster. The more powerful the spell, the greater the cost. That's what Nyna always told him. Could that explain him?

There were two walking and moaning corpses standing next to the gnome. Their flesh was rotting off their bones. Galin blinked. Could they be zombies? Like he heard about at school?

The gnome threw up his hands. "Why do I even bother? You idiots can't speak."

The liches passed right by the gnome and entered the cave, ignoring the gnome.

He rubbed his chin. "There must be a priestess of Odella nearby." He smiled. "I haven't fought someone in a long time, this will be fun." The gnome hurried inside the cave.

Galin just stared at the cave entrance. There were just the two zombies left and whatever waited for them inside. He moved back to the group, huddling around the corner. "There's two zombies, and the summoner is a gnome."

Ellis sighed. "We're fighting a midget mage? You've got to be kidding me."

"Shut up," Brock whispered.

Galin looked at Keya. "Can Zombies be killed?"

Keya nodded. "Just sever their heads from their bodies." She leaned in. "Like all summoned creatures, if we kill the summoner, all of the animated creatures that he summoned will die."

"So, the summoner is the key," Galin said. He smiled at Brock. "Ready?"

Brock smiled. "Yes, sire."

With his sword at the ready, Galin moved towards the entrance. As soon as the torchlight was visible, Galin charged towards the zombie on the left. Brock lunged at the one on the right.

The left zombie slashed its clawed hand at Galin.

In one motion, Galin stepped left while swinging his sword completely around, taking off the zombie's head.

Brock's sword crashed into the zombie's shoulder. He yanked on it, but couldn't get it out.

The zombie lunged at him with both clawed hands flailing towards his throat.

Jena leaped from behind Brock and severed the creature's head from its body with one blow of her short sword. She watched the zombie crash to the ground.

Brock put his foot on its chest and pulled his sword from its chest. "Thanks."

Ellis pointed up at the sky. "What's that?"

The rest of them looked up. High up in the sky, a fiery cloud was forming. Not a black storm cloud, but one that was as bright as the embers in a fire. It was growing and moving towards them.

Brock's face went white as he stared at Keya. "Is it?"

One ball of fire plunged to the ground, exploding on impact. The underbrush and dead trees ignited. It was followed by another, and another, and another.

"Get inside!" Galin yelled. They all followed him into the cave.

Tasar, a mere one hundred yards away, smiled. "Now, it's your turn, gnome." He disappeared into the darkness.

GALIN PRESSED against the wall of the cave, right next to the entrance. He counted everyone as they passed him, ensuring that everyone made it. "What the hell was that?"

Brock's face was still white. "I've seen that before, when I was on the wall with Thea the Loyal at

Staerdale Castle, just before the walls came down. But, she's dead."

"Who?" Keya asked.

"Beldroth. She was a pyromancer," Brock said.

Galin shook his head. "No, Father, there are lots of Dark Elf pyromancers."

"It can't be the gnome," Brock said. "When Beldroth did it, she had to keep her eyes on the castle. As soon as she looked away, it stopped. He's somewhere inside."

Ellis laughed. "Please, relax people. Let's go get *stubby* and then deal with that clown after. Too easy." He twirled his daggers in his hands. "Coming?"

Galin nodded. "Yeah. Father, could you take up the rear with Keya?"

"Sure," Brock replied.

Jena was next to Galin with her short sword drawn. "I will be a healer someday."

Galin smiled. "I know."

Ellis kicked Galin in the butt. "Come on already, we're wasting time. Do that crap after you're married."

The cave before them was well lit by torches mounted in sconces at every turn. The slightest sounds echoed through the cave. Light glistened off the moisture of the walls. Galin's soft leather boots slightly sank into the sandy floor.

Galin crept forward. Could he really do this? This was no test that Nyna could stop when they were losing. If someone dies here, they die. Nothing he could do about it. A cool breeze delivered the foul stench of rotting meat to his nostrils. He covered his nose and started breathing through his mouth.

They came to an intersection. Galin looked through the opening to the right. The liches, still glowing from Keya's spell, were pressed against the far wall, as if afraid of them. "They're no danger," Galin said.

"Let's get out of here before they are," Jena said as she tightened her grasp on the short sword.

Ellis grunted at the terrified liches. "Good thing, for *them!*"

Galin rolled his eyes. "Come on, Ellis."

"What did I say?" Ellis asked with a smile.

Galin and Jena moved past the opening, further down the cave. It was clear that the gnome didn't mind living in a hole in the ground. If they ran into more liches, what were they to do?

THE BLACK ROBED gnome rushed into a large cavern. The ceiling was covered with stalactites, like daggers hanging overhead. The rocky floor was uneven, and stalagmites sporadically protruded from the cave floor. The mica in the rock reflected the firelight from the sconces sprinkled throughout the cavern. "Where are you, my servants?"

The clanking of bones, as if assembling together, echoed throughout the cavern. One by one, twenty in all, fleshless humanoid creatures with green, glowing eyes approached him. "Yes, Master Balan," they said in unison.

Balan grinned. "We have intruders. Make sure they find their way in here." He looked towards the back of the cave and smiled. "It's time to try out my new pet."

Half of the skeletons hid amongst the stalagmites and the others ran out of the cavern.

GALIN STOPPED. The tunnel came to a fork just ahead. Which way? These tunnels could go on for miles underground. If they took the wrong path, they could be lost forever.

"Do we split up?" Jena asked?

Galin shook his head. "No, no way. But, which way?"

Ellis rolled his eyes. "Come on." He pulled out a coin. "Flip it? Heads left and tails right?"

Brock frowned. "Are you really going to let this idiot decide for you, *sire?*"

Ellis tossed the coin in the air.

Galen snatched it away. "No, I'm not." He threw the coin down the left tunnel.

"Damn it!" Ellis yelled. "That was mine."

"Everyone, quiet. Let's listen," Galin said. He closed his eyes. Nyna told them that sometimes you could see things with magic, but he didn't know how to do it with dragon magic, if it could be done at all. Tadus School of Magic taught him that focusing and controlling emotions made dragon magic work. What if he tried to see the gnome? What thoughts and emotions would he need to conjure up such a vision? How would he recognize it as a magical vision rather than his imagination?

"Look out!" Brock yelled.

Galen's eyes flashed open. Seven cackling man-sized skeletons with glowing, green eyes carrying swords, axes, and shields were charging at them from the left tunnel.

The lead skeleton swung its ax at Brock.

He sidestepped while swinging his sword at its mid-section.

The skeleton batted away Brock's sword and advanced on him.

Ellis threw a dagger at another skeleton's head; it embedded in its skull.

The skeleton smiled at Ellis.

"Oh, this sucks!" Ellis yelled as he backed away, looking for another weapon.

The tingle ran from Galin's heart. The tiny electrical arcs leaped across his skin and along his sword. His eyes began to glow as he charged in, with Jena right behind him. He swung his sword at the skeleton attacking Brock.

The skeleton raised its ax.

Galin severed its head from its fleshless body. The reanimated skeleton fell to pieces.

Jena swung at another one.

It blocked her.

Jena spun around. Her sword severed its backbone. It collapsed to the ground.

Ellis grabbed a fallen femur. "This will work."

The skeleton with the dagger embedded in its skull raised its sword.

Ellis swung the bone like a club. His new weapon shattered its right arm and the sword fell to the ground. Ellis grinned. "Who's laughing now?" He crushed the skeleton's skull, killing it.

Galin's glowing sword cut through two more in one swipe.

With both short swords drawn, Keya rushed at another. She swung both swords parallel to each other, severing both the skeleton's head and backbone simultaneously.

Brock slammed the last one into the wall, causing it to drop its sword. In a single movement, Brock side-stepped and slammed his sword into the skeleton's neck. The headless body dropped to the ground.

A cackle echoed down the tunnel ahead of them.

Galin gripped his sword tight. "Let's go."

THREE SKELETONS RAN into the huge cavern where Balan was waiting. "Master, they are coming."

Balan smiled. "Time to bring out the chimera."

A TINY DROP fell from the stalactite onto Galin's face. "Look," he said, pointing at the large opening into a well-lit cavern.

"What are we waiting for?" Ellis asked. "You are always stopping and looking and listening. Just go."

Brock shook his head. "No, there's no more cackling. There's something wrong. I've got a bad feeling."

"A trap?" Galin asked.

Keya nodded. "Yeah, I think so."

"What do we do?" Jena asked.

Galin smiled. "We spring it."

Ellis rolled his eyes. "Hurry up already," he said as he rushed inside with daggers in each hand.

"Bastard," Galin said as he chased after him.

Ellis laughed as he twirled his daggers in his hands. "I knew it! Cowards."

Keya looked around. "I…I don't understand."

Jena, with her sword drawn, moved next to Galin. "Where are they?"

Galin moved forward. "Did we go the right way?" He led everyone further into the immense cavern. Stalactites decorated the ceiling. Throughout the cavern floor were islands of stalagmites. Torches, mounted inside sconces, lined the walls. The further they moved inside, the more spread out they got.

A mass of cackling suddenly erupted from behind them.

Galin whipped around. Thirteen skeletons with glowing eyes cut off their escape. Their bones were slightly green and their eyes were a bright blue. "Are these different?"

Ellis looked down at his daggers. "This sucks." He immediately started looking around for another weapon.

Jena looked right at Keya. "Mother, can I do that spell you did before?"

Keya's mouth dropped. "I don't think it will work on these. These are not normal skeletons."

Galin moved forward. "We can do this." He focused his anger. The tiny electrical arcs jumped across his skin. His sword began to glow. Galin raised his sword and charged in.

Jena, with her short sword at the ready, ran towards the skeletons.

Eight skeletons charged straight at Galin and Jena with their axes and swords raised. The remaining five stayed back near the only exit.

As one skeleton swung at Brock, he dropped to ground. In a single motion Brock kicked the feet from underneath it and slammed the hilt of his sword into its skull, smashing it to pieces.

Jena leaped at the skeleton who thrust its sword towards Keya. "Mother!" She batted it away.

Keya slammed her two short swords on its right shoulder, cutting right through its spine. It collapsed on the ground.

"What the hades?" Ellis said as threw a dagger at a skeleton. It went right through its right eye socket and embedded itself into the back of its skull.

The skeleton raised its ax and charged at Ellis.

"This really sucks!" Ellis yelled as he tackled the skeleton, slamming it on the ground.

As soon as the skeleton hit the ground, the ax flew from its grip.

Ellis snatched it up and split the skeleton's skull in half. He spun it around in his hand. "I could get used to this one."

Galin's glowing sword sliced two skeletons in half with ease.

"Roar!" a deep raspy voice echoed throughout the cavern.

The skeletons jumped back.

Galin whipped around.

It had a lion's head with a scorpion-like tail and a dragon body. Its enormous body had a bright-blue glow, just like the skeletons' eyes.

Brock hacked off the head of another skeleton.

Ellis slammed his ax into the side of another. "Galin, we'll get these, while you get that."

Jena looked at her mother.

"I'm with you," Keya said as she moved next to her daughter.

"What is it?"

"The gnome summoner must be around here somewhere," Keya said. "Those are not undead."

Ellis picked up his daggers. "I'll find him, while you distract that," he said, pointing at the chimera. He disappeared around a stalagmite.

Brock broke another one. "Keya, help me."

Keya's sorrowful eyes looked right at Jena. "I'm sorry." She rushed to Brock's side.

Galin and Jena moved towards the chimera.

"What do we do?" Jena asked.

Galin shook his head. "Nyna always said think defense first."

"And that means what?"

Galin grinned. "Follow me." He focused his rage towards the creature, even more than he did with the skeletons. His skin glowed brighter and his sword became almost a bright white. He rushed in on its left.

Jena, with her short sword at the ready, charged in on the right.

The chimera's right claw backhanded Galin into a stalagmite, knocking off the top.

Jena slammed her short sword into its right front leg. Her sword bounced off its leg, as if it was made of solid rock. "It's not real!"

Galin shook his head. His mouth dropped as the chimera's scorpion-like tail reeled back. "Jena!" Its stinger slammed into her leg. Her blood spewed on the cavern floor as the chimera retrieved its stinger. His heart pounded. He had to save her.

"Jena!" Keya yelled as she charged towards her daughter.

"Sire, watch out!" Brock yelled.

The chimera's left claw swiped at him.

He sidestepped and slashed it with his glowing sword. Nothing. It bounced off. There must be a way to kill it! Must be! That's the only way he could save Jena.

The stinger bore down on Galin.

He batted it aside with his sword. More power, he must summon more power. His anger turned to rage, his rage turned into hatred. The white arcs dancing along his skin turned red. He felt his skin burning, but he didn't care.

The chimera smacked Keya away. She hit her head on a rock, knocking her unconscious.

Galin looked over at Keya.

As its claw swiped at Galin, his sword nicked its claw. He couldn't keep this up. His skin was on fire. Black spots started to appear. *Must calm down, I must control it.* He willed his power back down.

After he killed the last skeleton, Brock rushed at the chimera.

"Over here!" Galin rolled to the side as the stinger came crashing down, missing him.

The chimera yanked on its stinger, but it was stuck into the rock.

Galin swung his white-glowing sword at the tail and it bounced off. He needed more power, but his body couldn't take it. "How do we kill it?"

It broke its stinger free from the rock and squared off with Galin.

Brock dodged its claw. "We've got to kill the summoner."

Ellis! Where was Ellis? Galin threw a rock at the chimera, hitting it square in the forehead. "Come here, stupid!" As soon as it started towards him, Galin ran deeper into the cavern. "Ellis?" He weaved between stalagmites as the three-legged creature lumbered after him. "Where is he?"

The chimera swiped at Galin. It missed and took out a stalagmite.

"Over here!" Ellis yelled. "He's got me!"

Galin bolted around a boulder, following Ellis' voice.

The chimera's stinger nearly hit Galin's foot.

Twenty yards away, Ellis was hogtied in the corner. Balan's face turned white as Galin charged at him.

The chimera leaped at Galin from behind the boulder.

Galin grabbed Balan by the shoulders, dropping both of them to the ground.

Its tail reeled back.

"Galin, watch out!" Ellis yelled.

Galin rolled over with Balan on top of him.

The chimera's stinger skewered the gnome. As his life left him, the chimera froze. Piece by piece, the rock chimera fell to the ground, turning to dust on impact.

He untied Ellis. "Jena's hurt." Galin ran back to Jena.

Keya was already leaning over Jena. Her spell component bag was already out. Tears flowed down her cheeks. "I can't cure her!"

Galin hoisted Jena into his arms. "Maybe someone at Vebaco can." He carried her out of the cave.

Tasar watched the small band ride towards Vebaco from behind a tree. He sighed. "Can't trust a gnome to do a Dark Elf's job." His thin lips curled. "Next time."

CHAPTER 7

River of Souls

Holding the unconscious Jena on his horse with one hand and the reins with the other, Galin never rode harder. As Vebaco came into sight, he pushed Thea even harder. He'd lost his parents; he'd lost his adoptive mother; he would not lose his bride to be. His sorrowful eyes glanced down at her reddened face. Was this his fault? Did his over-confidence bring her to this? She trusted him, but he'd failed her. Tears rolled down his cheeks.

"Get her to the Lazy Spoon," Brock said. "I'll get the local healer. They might be able to help her."

Galin nodded.

Brock cracked the reins and bolted into town, with Keya in tow.

Ellis looked over at his friend. "We'll save her. I promise."

Galin yanked Thea to turn left into the Lazy Spoon. He leaped off his horse and tied her onto the hitching post.

Ellis ran inside.

"We're here, Jena," Galin said as pulled her off Thea. "I've got you." When her face touched his, his eyes widened. Her skin was hot to the touch. He carried her inside.

As soon as Galin entered the tavern, two patrons rushed to help him. The others pushed three tables together and the bartender rushed into the back. Galin laid Jena on the tables.

Sweat poured off her forehead. "Where? Where am…I?"

Galin's heart was breaking. He forced a smile on his face. "We're back at the Lazy Spoon. Your mom's getting some help."

Jena's sweet eyes looked right through him. "Did we…get him?"

"Yeah, we got him." Galin wiped the tears from his eyes. "You were great."

"What happened?" asked the bartender as he handed Ellis a damp towel.

"She was stung by one of the summoner's creatures," Ellis said as he placed the towel across Jena's forehead.

Jena looked right into Galin's eyes. "Am I going to die?"

Tears flowed like a vast river down Galin's face. His voice quivered. "No, I won't let you."

Jena's eyes began to fade. "I wish I was married before I…die." Her head fell to the side.

Those words hurt Galin worse than a sword through the gullet. Every time she wanted to, he was too busy. The worst part about it was that he'd asked her. He couldn't let her die. No, not now, not ever. He'd keep his promise to her. Galin kissed her forehead. "I love you."

"Make a hole!" Brock yelled as his pushed his way through the crowd.

Father? He was getting a healer. Galin's head snapped up. "She's gotten worse."

Brock and Keya moved aside.

An old woman carrying a staff with a large green stone at the top leaned over Jena. She wore a rope as a belt around her worn, brown robe. A small pouch hung from her left hip. "Where was she stung?"

"Her leg," Galin said. "What's your name?"

"Mia," the old woman said as tore Jena's trousers around the wound. "Oh my."

The flesh around the wound was turning black. Galin blinked. "Is it…spreading?"

Mia nodded. "Yes. Be quiet a moment." She pulled out a root from her pouch and rubbed it around the black skin. Her eyes were closed as she uttered inaudible words.

"What's she doing?" Ellis whispered

Keya shook her head. "This isn't any magic that I know."

Jena's leg started to glow. The black skin stopped spreading.

"Did you cure her?" Galin asked.

"I can't cure her," Mia said. "I don't have the right spell component."

"Jena, I'm so sorry," Galin said as hugged the unconscious Jena.

"What did you do?" Keya asked.

"Aren't you a healer? A Priestess of Odella? I stopped it from spreading," Mia said. "Well, at least for a while."

Galin's tearful eyes looked up. "Is there a cure?"

Mia frowned. "Yes, but it's impossible, especially now."

"What is?" Galin demanded. "I'll do anything to save Jena." He grabbed Mia's robe. "Anything, tell me, please."

"It requires the tongue of a black zombie," Mia said. "She has Withering Poisoning. It can only be contracted by certain types of summoned creatures."

Galin let Mia go. "Where do I get it?"

"There is a place in the Frog Woods, across the river of souls and north of Fison, it's called the Black Crypt. It used to be a monastery for Methos, the god of shadows," she said. "Legend has it that they cared more for the money made from their beer and wine than their god. He cursed them and turned them into the black zombies."

"How come I've never heard of them before?" Brock asked.

"Legend also says that they are confined to their

monastery for eternity." Mia looked away. "This is not the first case we've seen here. We sent at least ten men to get a tongue and none have returned."

"Why did you send them for only one?" Keya asked.

Mia smiled. "The tongue is not consumed in the healing spell."

Keya's tearful eyes turned towards Brock. "Please, help my daughter. Help me."

Brock hugged her. "Okay."

Galin shook his head. "No, I'll do it."

"Sire," Brock began, "you can't. You've got a duty."

Rage poured out of Galin's eyes. "To hell with my duty! Without Jena, life is…meaningless. Can you teach Keya the healing spell?" Galin asked Mia.

Mia nodded.

"Father, stay with Keya and Jena. Ellis and I will get the tongue," Galin said.

Brock bit his lip.

"Whoa, I never volunteered," Ellis said.

Galin glared at him. "You want her to die? Jena?"

"No, but…I should stay with Jena, to protect her," Ellis said. "I'm not going."

Galin's face reddened and his eyes began to glow.

Ellis put his hands up. "All right, I'll go. Don't have an ogre." He smirked at Galin. "I guess I can save your ass again."

Mia rubbed her chin. "A human male that can use magic. Are you the one…they're scared of?"

Galin nodded. "I am." He looked right at Brock with his puffy eyes. "Right after I get the tongue and we cure Jena, I'll resume my duty. Okay?"

Brock nodded. "Okay. I'll make sure that mayor keeps his part of the deal and I'll meet you in Nia."

"Where's that?" Ellis asked.

"South of Frog Woods and along the road to Plaka and Grurg, just west of the Wailing Mountains." Brock put his hand on Galin's shoulder. "There is, or was, a Darkstrider checkpoint near the entrance to the Wailing Mountains. Avoid it."

Galin nodded. "I will, Father." He kissed Jena. "I'll see you soon." Galin motioned to Ellis. "Let's go."

"Can't we eat first?" Ellis asked.

"Wait a minute," the bartender said as he rushed into the back room.

"You need your strength," Brock said.

The bartender emerged with a full medium sack. He tossed it to Ellis. "Here, take this. There is enough food for about a week."

"Great, thank you," Galin said as he snatched the bag from Ellis. "Come on. We'll eat on the way."

Ellis followed Galin out the door.

GALIN PATTED Thea as they rode across the pasture. The sun crept over the Wailing Mountains like an early morning yawn. They'd been riding for hours, but he didn't care. Jena was depending on him. What if she died? How many times, after he asked her to marry him, did he say that now was not the right time? How many times did he turn her away? Was it really because

Brock or Nyna told him to, or was it because he was afraid?

Ellis tossed another piece of bread into his mouth. "This is good."

Galin glared at him. "That's all we have for the week."

Ellis grinned. "Yeah, we'll eat good for a few days and I'll grab us some grub for the last two. We'll be fine. Stop worrying."

Galin's stone eyes looked ahead. "I can't stop worrying."

Ellis looked away. "Don't act like you're the only one who cares about her. I'm her friend, too."

Ellis was right. Galin swallowed. "I'm sorry. It's my fault."

"How?" Ellis asked. "You didn't sting her and get her sick, that *thing* did that."

Galin cocked an eye at Ellis. "Yeah, but she wouldn't have even been there if it wasn't for me. She'd be safe...*somewhere*." Would she? Would she, really? He turned away from Ellis. Yeah, of course she would. Maybe, if he married back at Crey Village...Maybe if he just ran away instead of trying to fulfill his adoptive father's dream, she'd be okay. Maybe. Maybe, not. He bit his lip.

Ellis shook his head. "You're being an orc's ass again. Stop being such a lout." He grinned. "You're not *that* stupid."

Galin laughed. "You're right; *you* are." His eyes softened as he looked over at Ellis. "Thanks."

Ellis moved Runt closer. "Someone has to keep you in line."

"Right," Galin said. The sounds of rushing water reached his ears. Ahead was the River of Souls. It was enormous. The white crests raced by them towards Methos Lake. Galin urged Thea to the shore. It must have been at least one hundred yards wide. He gazed upon the raging waters. "Can't get across this way."

Ellis nodded. "Yeah, let's follow the shoreline. Maybe we'll get lucky."

"Sure," Galin said as he cracked the reins.

They rode until it was close to dinner time. The seemingly endless river only got wider the further they went. As the sun sank, Galin grew more tired. "Let's stop for the night." He jumped down from Thea's back and pulled out her feedbag from the saddlebags.

Ellis did the same. "I'll do the cooking," he said as he grabbed the sack filled with food.

Galin grinned. "The baker's son? About time you did something."

An hour later, Galin's nose wrinkled as the smell of gruel cooking over the fire invaded his nostrils. He pinched his nose. "Really? I hate that stuff."

Ellis scooped some into a tin bowl and passed it over to Galin. "You haven't tried mine."

"Okay," he said as he put a spoonful in his mouth. Galin spit it out. "This sucks!"

Ellis laughed. "What did you expect? It's gruel."

Galin smiled. "Well, I guess we can't be too picky."

"Unless you're me."

As he put another spoonful in his mouth, he

thought of Sally. She used to feed this *stuff* to him every day. But, that was before they killed her. Every time he thought of something good about his adoptive mother, it was tainted by what they did to her. He couldn't save her, but now he was supposed to save Jena? What if the prophecy was wrong? What if he wasn't the one? What if he couldn't live up to everyone else's expectations?

Ellis tossed his bowl at Galin. "I cooked, you clean. Night." He pulled out a blanket and laid down near the fire.

"I'll take the first watch," Galin said as he headed towards the river.

GALIN FELT a sharp pain in his side.

"Hey, get up," Ellis said.

The bright sun hurt Galin's eyes as they cracked open. "Damn, what time is it?"

Ellis shook his head as he put the sack of food into Runt's saddlebags. "No idea, but it's later than we were supposed to get moving." He grinned at him. "Damn, *you* overslept."

As Galin sat up, the thin wool blanket fell off his chest. He stretched. "Yeah, let's get going. Jena's depending on us."

"How do we get across that?" Ellis asked as he pointed at the River of Souls.

Galin mounted Thea. "Keep moving up the river and look for a boat?" He urged his mount along the shoreline.

When Ellis caught up to Galin, he said, "There must be a bridge somewhere."

"We'll see."

As the afternoon sun climbed high in the sky, Galin wiped the sweat from his brow. "Look," he said, pointing ahead. An old dock stuck out into the river like a breakwater. There was a single boat tied off onto the dock, but it was a small boat. Near the shoreline was an old man sitting by a fire with a spit rotating over the flames.

Ellis took in the aroma. "Rabbit? I bet it's rabbit."

"Are you always hungry?" Galin asked.

Ellis grinned. "Always." He urged Runt towards the old man.

When Galin joined Ellis by the old man, he dismounted. Ellis was already munching on a rabbit leg. "Afternoon. I'm Galin," he said as he shook the old man's hand.

"I'm William," the old man said. His skin was wrinkled around his deep-blue eyes and there was a long scar down his right cheek. He held out a piece of rabbit. "Want some?"

Galin took the chunk of meat as he plopped down next to Ellis. "Thanks." He looked at the sailboat tied off onto the dock. "Where are you going?"

William shook his head. "Just got back from Methos Lake. I was making a delivery to Tadus School of Magic for a merchant friend of mine." The breeze whipped through his thin, gray hair. "I live in Iprand, just a few miles that way," William said as he pointed southwest. He plopped a piece of meat into his mouth. "Why do you ask?"

Ellis swallowed. "We're trying to cross the river."

William looked over at Thea and Runt and frowned. "My boat's too small to carry horses."

Galin's heart sank.

"Where's the closest bridge or another boat?" Ellis asked.

"The bridge is only about another mile or so up the road." William leaned forward. "But, there's a Darkstrider checkpoint on both sides of the bridge. Be careful, those orcs don't need a reason to snatch you up."

Galin stood up. "Sounds like we've got no choice."

Ellis glared at him. "Two Darkstrider checkpoints on both sides of the bridge? We can't go there. What if they recognize us?"

William cocked his head. "Recognize you? Who are you two?"

Galin looked away. "Just a couple of kids they're looking for."

William frowned. "I see. Good luck."

"Thanks for the rabbit," Ellis said as he mounted Runt. He followed Galin further down the riverbank.

"How do we cross the bridge?" Galin asked.

Ellis laughed. "Easy, just act like you belong there."

Galin nodded. "Right." They rode for another ten minutes before the bridge came into sight. It was a long stone bridge with three pillars coming out of the water. The stones were not polished, but used to be. It was two hundred yards long, with Darkstriders at each end. Why both sides? Did they check you going on and getting off? *No, no way. They must be checking travelers as they entered the bridge. Anything else didn't make sense, right? The center of the bridge was at least twenty feet above the water; why would they think someone would jump out of the river onto the bridge, rather than just swimming underneath it? They wouldn't, right?*

"Hide your sword," Ellis said as he slipped his daggers into Runt's saddlebags.

"Got it." Galin's sword was in a sheath attached to the saddle. He slid it under the saddle blanket.

"Just act natural," Ellis said. He grinned. "Not like when we stole those apples back in Crey Village."

Galin glared at Ellis. "I can do it." He urged Thea towards the checkpoint. There was nothing special about it. The checkpoint was the Darkstriders blocking the way of travelers before they crossed the bridge. But the Darkstriders guarding the bridge were not humans or Dark Elves, they were Feral Orcs. They were more gray than green. Their toes were clawed and their oversized hands were patting each other's back, as if they were telling each other jokes. Galin's eyes focused on the stacked weapons just off to the side of them. Maybe Ellis was right. They weren't on edge, attacking the next poor traveler that happened to walk by. No, they were—barely paying attention.

Ellis and Galin rode side by side as they approached the checkpoint. "Let me do the talking," Ellis said.

Three unarmed Feral Orcs blocked the bridge. The largest one had long, black hair pulled back. "Halt! State your name and business in the next district!" it said.

Ellis' thin lips curled. "We're both sons of the fish monger in Nia. We're returning home. I'm Paul and this is Billy," he said, pointing at Galin.

Another of the orcs stepped forward, rubbing its chin. "You look—familiar."

"We've never met," Galin said. Were they caught?

The orc shook his head. "No, that's not it."

The larger one hesitated.

Ellis started laughing. "Let me guess, all us humans look alike? Come on, you can do better than that." He reached into his saddlebags and pulled out the sack of food. He tossed them three loaves of sourdough bread. "Here, have some lunch on us."

The larger orc smiled as he bit into the loaf of bread. "Okay, let them through."

Galin's eyes focused ahead of them, not even looking into their eyes as they passed the first check-point. With each step towards the other side, he felt more relieved and the more he prayed about them not checking travelers going off the bridge. They were almost to the other side.

"Stop them!" yelled an orc from the checkpoint they'd just passed. "They're wanted!"

"Oh crap," Ellis said.

The three unarmed orcs on the far side charged at them.

Galin grinned at Ellis. "They're unarmed; try to keep up." He cracked reins and Thea bolted across the bridge.

Both Runt and Thea raced towards the orcs, side by side.

The orcs spread out, blocking the bridge.

Galin cracked his reins, again.

Ellis followed suit.

The two mares crashed into the Feral Orcs.

Thea knocked the orc on the right off the bridge and trampled the one in the center.

Runt knocked the last orc off the bridge into the raging waters below.

"Quick, Frog Woods is just ahead!" He veered Thea due north, bent on reaching the town of Fison. He cracked the reins, urging Thea to move even faster.

"Damn it, Galin! Runt's named Runt for a reason," Ellis yelled. "Slow down."

Galin looked back. Nothing, no Darkstriders. "We've lost them."

"Well, duh," Ellis said. "They didn't have mounts."

"Come on." Galin led Ellis into the Frog Woods. *Is that the reason they lost them?*

CHAPTER 8

The Black Crypt

droplet of water splashed onto Galin's face. The trees were covered with green moss like a rash. Their leaves were so thick they nearly blotted out the sun. As soon as the boys entered Frog Woods, they were cold, almost as if the heat from the sun couldn't penetrate the thick, sickly looking trees.

"Is it going to rain?" Ellis asked.

Galin shook his head. "No, it's the air. It's so...so moist."

Thea stopped.

"What is it, girl?" Galin asked as he patted her head.

Ellis looked around. "I don't like this place. It's... creepy." He pointed at Thea. "Even your dumb horse senses it."

A wolf howled in the distance. Galin's stomach twisted. "It's in your head." He urged Thea forward.

Runt ducked under a branch, but Ellis wasn't so lucky. The branch slapped him in the face. "Damn you!"

Galin laughed. He heard a moan amongst the rustling leaves. The hairs on the back of his neck stood up at attention.

Thea stopped.

"Is it still in my head?" Ellis asked. "You do remember that we are looking for a black zombie, right?"

Galin nodded. "I didn't forget." Even the Infernal Grotto wasn't like this. It was almost like the whole Frog Woods was cursed, not just those poor creatures in the Black Crypt. "Let's keep going."

Ellis shivered. "Fine."

A MERE HUNDRED yards behind them, a black-robed Dark Elf rode a brown horse. Tasar pulled the hood off his head. "Where are you going?" he asked. He reached into his saddlebags and pulled out a small pouch. It contained a clear crystal within the grasp of a dragon made of gold on the end of a golden chain. He slipped it around his neck. It had a faint dark-blue glow. The dark woods were no longer dark to his eyes. He could see through the darkness as if the sun was at its peak during the brightest day.

"That's better," Tasar said. He urged his mount forward, following Galin and Ellis, but far enough back that they couldn't see him. If it didn't have to be an accident or at least not look like an assassination, he'd be done already. This should have been an easy 300,000 crowns. He sniffed. The whole idea of fearing a martyr was foolish. The Darkstriders were in control of the kingdom and nothing was going to stop them. Sure, they really didn't go east of the Wailing Mountains, but why bother? Everything of value was in Axain, not Ithsein to the east or Shumnar or Leonga to the north. But, Tasar had no loyalty to them. Why not use them like they used every other Dark Elf in Setan and Volor? Being an independent contractor had its…advantages.

Tasar veered his steed to the right, following Galin and Ellis. What was it about this boy? Sure, he was supposedly the prophesied boy king that would destroy the Darkstriders, but could he? Sure, the boy had powers, but he had no army. Even an army of 10,000 men couldn't take Staerdale Castle. The Darkstriders only pulled it off because they'd already infiltrated the castle by assuming human form for decades, but the boy wouldn't have that much time. No, it would have to be a straight-out attack. Tasar shook his head. This boy and his allies were feared way too much, but he'd be more than willing to take the Darkstrider's crowns for these jobs. He rubbed his chin. What if the prophecy was wrong?

ORANGE LIGHT of a sunset seeped through the tress ahead. As Galin and Ellis moved closer, the brighter the light became. "Are we coming to a clearing?" Galin asked.

Ellis gripped his reins tighter. "I hope so."

Galin looked over at Ellis. "Me too." Ever since they were kids, Galin (back when his name was Seth), Jena, and Ellis were like siblings. Ellis was always the one who lightened things up and took more risks than Galin liked, but he was always there for him. No matter what Galin asked him to do, Ellis always stepped up. Was this loyalty? Once he raised an army, would they be as loyal to him as Ellis? How does one so young get men to do things that would probably get them killed? How does—?

"What are you thinking over there?" Ellis asked.

Galin shook his head. "I'm just—well, after we save Jena, we're getting back to raising an army."

"Yeah, no kidding."

"What do I know about leading an army? Nothing." Galin looked away. "I don't know that even *I* would follow me."

Ellis glared at him. "Will you knock off the self-pity crap, please! You make me want to puke all over you." He grinned. "I won't miss, either."

"Why do you follow me?"

Ellis sniffed. "I don't. You're my friend, and so is Jena. That's why I'm here." He laughed. "Believe me, you're no great leader."

"What if I fail the people who decide to follow because of that…prophecy?" Galin asked.

Ellis shrugged. "So, what if they do? I mean, if they are really that stupid then they—"

"They really believe it, Ellis."

"I know," Ellis said. "Galin, you can only do the best you can. Listen to those who have more experience than you, but don't blindly follow their advice, either."

Galin shook his head. "How will I know the difference?"

Ellis glared at him. "How the hell would I know? I'm just a thief from Crey Village. Stop being so damn gushy on me, before I kick your ass."

They entered a large clearing. The wind rustled the tall grass covering the valley floor for as far as the eye could see. The Wailing Mountains were visible to the west. In the center was a hill with a large manor on top. It was covered with vines, as if unkempt for years, or even decades—or even longer. The sun was setting over the mountains.

"That must be it," Galin said.

Ellis stopped Runt at the wood line. "Let's camp here and go in the morning."

Galin frowned. "Why? Jena needs it now!"

"Because were going after black zombies, dimwit! Do you really want to do that in the dark?" Ellis demanded. "That would be stupid. Besides, if we get killed, Jena will die too. We need to be smart about it."

Galin dismounted Thea. "Fine. I guess you have a point." They began to set up camp.

Tasar dismounted. "The black crypt? Another opportunity?" he asked himself.

~

THE MORNING CAME QUICKLY. As soon as the sun peeked over the horizon, Galin shook Ellis. "Let's go."

Ellis was covered by a wool horse blanket, using his pack as a pillow. "I'm coming," Ellis said as he sat up.

Galin started packing up their camp. "Do zombies come out during the day?"

Ellis shook his head. "How the hell would I know? I never knew these freaky things even existed." He put the last of his things into Runt's saddlebags.

"Ready?" Galin asked as he mounted Thea.

Ellis nodded.

Galin urged Thea out into the long grass, heading towards the vine-covered manor. His stomach twisted as they got closer. His eyes jumped from rock to rock, mound to mound, to anything that a black zombie could hide behind. He blinked. What does a black zombie even look like? Was it like a lich? Like those things in the Infernal Grotto? In his rush, Galin didn't even think to ask what they even looked like. Only one thing was for sure, they were not outside the manor. In fact, there was nothing.

"Maybe they sleep inside or something during the day," Ellis said.

Galin shrugged. He stopped Thea in front of the manor. Not only was it covered with vines, the stones were chipped and stained with blood. No grass grew within ten feet of its walls. It was almost like the plants were cursed, too. The solid walls came to two large solid wood doors. They were covered by elaborate carvings. A century ago, they must have been beautiful, but not anymore. The left door was closed and the right door was pushed inward, hanging off the bottom hinge. "What happened?"

Ellis shook his head. "No idea." He tied Runt off and grabbed his daggers and a small sack. "Let's get this thing and get out of here."

Galin drew his sword. He willed the dragon magic to be ready and he felt the familiar tingle in his heart. "Come on."

Ellis Followed Galin inside.

As if the smell was held within the manor's walls by some magical spell, the stench of decaying bodies ambushed Galin. The courtyard was huge. Nothing grew on the ground, not even a single blade of grass. Galin looked around at the empty courtyard. Across the yard were six old wine barrels stacked against the main house. The stone manor house was two stories tall and looked a thousand years old. Near the far wall was a pile of broken wooden crates.

Ellis grabbed his nose. "This place smells like you."

Galin glared at him. "Funny. Let's clear the courtyard before we go inside."

"Sure." Ellis walked to Galin's left.

Galin started towards the barrels. Since the courtyard was empty, there were only two places a zombie could hide, right? His grip tightened. His head snapped left as a crate was knocked over. He pointed over at the pile of crates.

Ellis nodded.

Galin willed his offensive dragon magic. Tiny electrical arcs leapfrogged across his skin and engulfed his sword. His eyes began to glow. *I can do it*, he thought.

Something moaned from behind the pile.

Ellis shifted further left, trying to envelop the creature.

Galin picked up the pace.

As it stood up, several crates were toppled off the pile. Its rotting flesh was as black as the night. Its exposed bones were even darker. Bright-green eyes decorated its dark skull. The clawed fingers matched the sharpened teeth. It charged at Galin.

Galin sidestepped, tripping it.

It rolled right.

Galin's sword slammed onto its right arm, severing it from the black zombie's body. He jumped back as the severed arm used its fingers to charge at him. "What the hell?" Galin kicked the arm away.

The severed limb landed near Ellis.

"Oh, damn!" Ellis said as the arm clawed its way towards him.

The zombie got back up, staring right into Galin's eyes.

Galin blinked. His began to feel heavy. His legs started to wobble.

"What are you doing?" Ellis yelled as he kicked the arm away. "Kill it already!"

Galin snapped out of it.

The zombie lunged at him, grabbing his arm.

Galin tried to pull away.

It pulled his arm towards its mouth.

"No you don't!" Galin yelled as he dropped to the

ground and immediately rolled to the left, leaving the zombie face down in the dirt.

It started to get back up.

In a single motion, Galin leaped to feet and brought his sword down, severing both of its legs.

The legs twitched, as if trying to move. The zombie grabbed Galin's foot with its last arm.

Galin kicked it away. He raised his sword.

The zombie rolled over onto its back.

His sword slammed into its neck, decapitating the creature.

Ellis snatched up the head.

It tried to bite him.

He tossed it to the ground. "How am I supposed to cut its tongue out? It's still alive!"

Galin smashed the headless body. "So's this thing."

Ellis looked around. He needed...something. A fallen piece of stone was laying on the ground near the pile of crates. He bolted towards it.

"What are you doing?" Galin asked as kicked the moving, headless body.

"I've got an idea," Ellis said as he picked up the rock.

Galin blinked as he saw the two legs crawl to its body. "I've got a bad feeling. Hurry!"

Ellis slammed the rock into its skull, ripping the jawbone from the skull. He snatched it up and kicked the skull away. "The tongue is still moving!"

Galin's mouth dropped as the two legs reattached themselves to the zombie. The closer severed arm pulled itself towards the headless creature. "Hurry, we can't kill it!"

Ellis carved out the tongue and tossed it into the small sack. "Got it."

Galin whirled around as he heard more moans behind them. There were at least ten to twelve black zombies emerging from the manor house. "We've got to go, now!"

Ellis bolted towards the doors. As soon as Runt was in sight, he leaped on her back.

Galin sheathed his sword and sprinted towards Thea.

"Come on!" Ellis yelled.

Galin climbed on Thea and cracked the reins. Thea galloped away from the manor with Runt close behind. As they approached the wood line, Galin looked back. "They're not following us."

"Maybe they can't leave the black crypt," Ellis said. He looked down at the small sack thrashing around inside the saddlebag. "That damn thing is still moving!"

Galin urged Thea forward. "Let's save Jena."

"After you," Ellis said.

Galin headed south, towards Nia. They would get there in time, *hopefully*.

CHAPTER 9

Save Jena

After hours of hard riding through the Frog Woods, Galin and Ellis reached the southern edge, just west of the Wailing Mountains. When Galin moved out of the woods, he smiled as the sun warmed his face. He pulled Thea's reins back, causing her to slowly come to a halt. "Five-minute break?" Galin asked.

The sweat on Ellis' face glistened in the light. He gulped some fresh air. "Sure, if you need to." He climbed down off of Runt's back.

Galin tied Thea off to a small tree. He laid his sword down next to him as he leaned against it. They rode hard through the Frog Woods and he could almost see the main road off in the distance. A cool breeze splashed over his face. Yeah, there was only one thing left between them and saving Jena; the checkpoint on the main road. Would it only have a few Darkstriders, like the bridge? Galin shifted in his seat as he looked around. There was forest behind; in fact, the trees were sprinkled in the grassland as far as the eye could see.

"What are we going to do about the checkpoint? If Brock is right, it should be just over the next rise," Ellis said. "I don't think we can go around it."

Galin frowned. "I was wondering that too." He pointed at the grassland ahead of them. "If we try to go around them, they'd see us. Could we be any more suspicious than that?"

Ellis shook his head. "Well, we could head back towards the bridge and cut east after we cross the road. It would take a little longer."

"A little? Are you serious? It would add at least another day," Galin said. "Jena may not have that long."

"You don't know that."

Galin glared at him. "No, I don't, but you don't know that she does, either." He stared at the barely visible building along the road in the distance. Did he have much choice? No, Jena was depending on him.

"Look," Ellis said as he pointed at a caravan, just coming over the bridge, moving towards the checkpoint.

"Good idea, we hide amongst them," Galin said.

Ellis mounted Runt. "Let's get in line."

As Galin climbed on Thea's back, he heard a loud crack, like a stick being broken underfoot. "What's that? A black zombie?" He drew his sword. "Something could be following us."

Ellis laughed. "You're pathetic. Now come on before we can't join that caravan." He cracked the reins and Runt galloped towards the caravan.

Galin looked back into the woods. Nothing. Maybe it was just his imagination. Thea raced to catch up with Runt. As they came closer to the passing caravan, Galin and Ellis slowed down and they fell in at the end. His adoptive mother once told him that to hide a flower, put it in a flower garden. How true was that? He was going to find out. The caravan must have had at least fifty people and twenty or so wagons to be inspected by the guards. Would the Darkstriders be so tired by the time they got to them that they would just let them pass? Would he? Maybe, maybe not.

"Think this will work?" Ellis whispered.

Galin tried to smile. "Of course it will." It had better, or they would never reach Jena in time. The caravan crawled along the road, approaching the checkpoint. Galin shifted Thea off to the side of the road to get a better look. The small building, he saw from the edge of the Frog Woods, was a stone gatehouse with walls extended at least two hundred feet towards the north and the south. Off to the left of the house, along the northern wall were at least six or seven Feral Orcs on their wolf mounts. Galin swallowed. "This is probably a mistake."

Ellis shook his head. "No, our best shot is to move along with the caravan."

"They're ready to chase someone," Galin said. "Can you guess who?"

Ellis grinned. "Yeah, kind of flattering, isn't it?"

Galin could see the fear on his face. He nodded. "I guess it is." Galin looked towards the right, towards Nia. They could break off, but the mounted Feral Orcs would surely chase them. There was probably more of them that he couldn't see. His stomach tumbled and twisted as the caravan entered the checkpoint.

"Here they come," Ellis said, pointing at the Feral Orcs walking down the line.

Galin swallowed. *Just act natural,* he told himself, *just act like I belong here.* The closer the orc got, the drier his mouth became.

The lead orc passed the cart in front of them and looked up. "Where are you going?"

Going? "Umm…Drusas," Galin said.

The orc shook its head. "What's your business in that goblin hole?"

Galin blinked.

"Visiting family," Ellis said. "Don't you do that?" He smiled at the Orc. "Ever been there? They've got a nice bakery in the market square."

The orc rolled its eyes as it yawned. He motioned to the orcs manning the gatehouse. "Let them through. They're cleared."

A wave of relief fell upon Galin as they passed through the gate. The farther he got from the checkpoint, the better he felt. Ahead, the road came to a fork.

"Which way to Nia?" Ellis asked.

"South," Galin said, "turn right." Galin led Ellis down the road towards Nia.

. . .

TASAR RODE across the field from the Frog Woods behind the checkpoint. When a Feral Orc yelled at him, he removed his hood and the orc cowed in fear. Tasar sighed. "To hell with making it look like an accident. It's time for a more…direct approach." His black hair turned blond and his deep-blue skin became white. He blinked. Tasar's eyes were no longer black, but a sea blue. His ears were no longer pointed. Tasar looked… human. "Time to end this." He rode after Galin and Ellis.

AFTER RIDING along the southern road for an hour, Galin and Ellis came across a series of long wooden fences around an enormous pasture. Cattle and sheep were munching on green grass. "We must be close," Galin said.

"How many are out there?" Ellis asked, pointing at the livestock.

Galin looked down the road. Over a small rise off in the distance, he could see the top of a temple of Odella. It was barely in sight, but it was there. "Come on," he said as he brought Thea to a gallop.

Ellis sighed. "Always in a hurry." He chased after Galin.

It was a mere ten minutes for Galin and Ellis to reach Nia. It was a poor and simple farming village. All of the houses had thatched roofs and their walls were made out of logs. There were no cobblestone roads in the village, only dirt.

Ellis held his nose. "Damn, even the town smells."

Galin frowned. "As if you don't stink, goblin ass." The aroma of fresh bread invaded his nostrils as they rode close to the market square. "Smell that?"

Ellis smiled as he closed his eyes. "Yeah, I do."

"It's almost like home," Galin said. The market square had a well in the center with several women collecting water in buckets. Surrounding the square were merchants selling off their wagons, everything from fruits to fish to clothing to magical components. Every building in the square was one story, save one. It was a three-story building with a porch in the front with four tables and stools surrounding each of them. Above the door was a picture of a wide-eyed owl with its wings spread, as if to flee from some predator. Underneath the owl were the words 'The Cowardly Owl' painted in orange. A large man with brown hair with streaks of gray sat amongst several younger and more muscular men. "That's Father!" Galin cracked the reins and headed towards his adoptive father.

Brock jumped down from the porch and ran towards Galin. As soon as Galin tied Thea to the hitching post, Brock hugged him. "I missed you," he said.

Galin shook off his adoptive father. "Jena? Are we too late?"

"No, follow me," Brock said as he ran inside.

Ellis grabbed the sack as he jumped down from Runt. "Wait for me!"

As soon as they entered the door, Brock veered left and went right up the stairs. "Here!" He opened the first door on the right and rushed inside, with Galin close behind.

Galin blinked as he saw Jena lying on the bed with her mother crying at her bedside. Jena's skin was soaked. Her hair looked like she just came out of the lake and…and her skin was dry and beginning to crack. Galin saw the pain in her face every time she took a breath. He knelt down next to her. "I'm here." Tears welled up behind his eyes. He bit his lip. "I'm…I'm so sorry."

Keya glared at him. "Do you have it?" she demanded.

Ellis handed Keya the sack with the still moving tongue inside. "Here."

He couldn't hold it back anymore. Tears started rolling down Galin's cheeks like the rushing waters of a fast-moving river. "Can you cure her? Please, by the gods, save her!" His head collapsed on her chest. "It's my fault. It's all my fault. I'm…I'm so sorry, Jena!"

Keya frowned. "Ellis, stay with me, I need help performing the ritual." She looked up at Brock. "Take him out of here. I only have one chance at this."

Brock nodded as he grabbed Galin by the shoulders. "Come on, son."

Galin wrested himself from Brock's grip. "No, I want to stay. I don't want to leave her again."

Ellis pushed Galin towards the door. "Do you want her to live? Then get the hell out!"

"He's right, son," Brock said as he pulled Galin through the door into the hallway.

"I'll come and find you when it's over," Ellis said as he closed the door.

Galin collapsed to the floor, sobbing. "Did you see her skin?"

Brock nodded as he knelt down next to his adoptive son. "I did." He sighed. "Vebaco sent us two hundred volunteers and—"

Galin pushed Brock away. "I don't want to talk about that now."

Brock shook him. "You have to talk about it. Their captain is downstairs and you need to get it together. Your age is part of the reason we are having a hard time recruiting fighters to our cause. The same cause, mind you, that most of them are already fighting."

"I don't care. All I want is Jena to be safe," Galin sobbed.

Brock slapped his left cheek. "You'd better care. Keya will heal her and if she can't, do you want Jena to die for nothing? Because if you lose those men, word will spread that you are a coward. Do you want that?"

"I don't care!"

"I do! I won't let Sally's death be in vain because of a snotty little hobgoblin who can't control himself," Brock said.

Galin blinked. The image of when they found her violated and tortured body in the bedroom flashed through his mind. He'd killed Shania, the Dark Elf responsible for her death...and nearly himself. He wiped his eyes. "Can Keya cure her?"

Brock nodded. "Now that she has the tongue." He helped Galin to his feet. "This would be a good time to figure out what exactly we are doing. It may keep your mind occupied. We have a real problem to figure out and not much time to do it in. What do you say?"

Galin wiped his eyes one last time. "Okay. Let's meet the captain."

"He's downstairs," Brock said.

Galin followed Brock down into the tavern below.

CHAPTER 10

Nia Strongman

Sweet music from the lute player on the far side of the tavern perked Galin's ears. Every stool around the bar was occupied, and bartender was rushing from one end to the other. Tables were sprinkled throughout the room. The wooden floor planks creaked as they walked towards a large round table in the corner. A burly man with soft-blue eyes was sitting at the table with his back to the wall. His long, brown hair hung down his back. He wore a soiled brown tunic. As Galin and Brock approached, he rose to his feet.

Brock took the seat next to man. "Galin, this is Val Lonsberry. He's the captain for the volunteers from Vebaco."

Galin shook Val's hand as he sat down. "Pleasure to meet you."

Val sat back down and took another swig of ale. "I brought two hundred men, sire."

Galin put his finger in front of his lips. "Shh, keep that down. Just call me Galin."

Val nodded.

"That's more than I expected," Galin said.

Brock waved over a beer wench. "It's not enough."

Galin rolled his eyes. "I know, but it's a start. We'll get more."

A young girl carrying a tray smiled at Galin. "What can I get for you?"

"Two ales, please," Brock said as he tossed two crowns on her tray.

"Be right back." She hurried towards the bar.

Brock leaned in. "I found some old friends on the way here."

Galin raised an eyebrow. "Old friends?"

Brock nodded. "They used to be knights under your father. They told me that there is an underground army being created in the shadows."

"Who?" Val asked. He glared at the blond-haired man sitting down at the next table over. "Should we move?"

Brock looked over at the blue-eyed man. "No, he doesn't look like trouble. Just keep our voices down."

Galin grabbed Brock's forearm. "When are they going to join us?"

Brock shifted in his seat. "That's just it. They're not."

"Why not?" Val asked.

"Well, they can't afford to follow the wrong man." Brock's face fell as he looked at Galin. "They've heard of the prophecy too, but they don't believe it. We need a victory to prove to them that you can lead them."

Galin frowned. "How? We need fighters to do that."

"If we do it, there is a rumor among them that the war mages in the Tower of the Shadow Mage may join us too," Brock said.

"Brock, he's right. How can we get a victory without fighters?" Val asked. "I—"

"Here you go," the beer wench said as she gave Galin and Brock each an ale. "Enjoy."

"Two hundred men are not enough to take anything big enough to prove his worth as a leader," Val said. He sighed. "Maybe this was a mistake."

Galin sipped his ale. How could he do it? What would it take to prove that he *really* was this great leader? Even if they got four hundred troops from here, it wouldn't be enough. Galin blinked. "What about getting volunteers from Nia?"

Brock sighed. "I've been asking around and the people are willing, but Brice Colon, the self-proclaimed lord of the manor, wouldn't allow it. Whatever the people earn from their blood and sweat, Brice takes three-fourths."

"Why do the people put up with it?" Galin asked.

Val frowned. "In real life, whoever can force their will on others makes all the rules."

"That makes no sense," Galin said. "What if they don't pay?"

"They regret it, physically," Brock replied.

"He's a bully then." Galin took a swig of ale. "Will they help us if we take care of it?"

Brock nodded. "We'll get a few hundred at least."

Galin looked directly into Brock's eyes. "Are you sure?"

"Yeah."

Val shook his head. "I still don't see how we could have a major victory with four to five hundred fighters."

"When we were coming back, we passed through the checkpoint near the Wailing Mountains. We could definitely take that out," Galin said.

"To what end?" Brock asked. "The Darkstriders would immediately send reinforcements. They would overrun us."

"There is an outpost that acts as the checkpoint on the other side of the mountains, just west of Drusas," Val said.

"It used to be an old keep, when your father was king." Brock rubbed his chin. "If we take it, we could block the Darkstriders from crossing the mountains and free the villages on the far side of the Wailing Mountains."

Val shook his head. "Not possible. Even if we had siege equipment, we just don't have enough fighters to take anything like that."

"Is it heavily manned?" Galin asked.

Brock shook his head. "I don't think so. Val's right, we can't attack a keep."

Galin glared at Brock. "Is there another target that we *can* attack?"

Brock shook his head. "Nothing big enough to bring them out of the shadows."

"Then we have no choice," Galin said. "First, we'll eliminate Brice Colon and give back the things he stole from these people. Then, we train our volunteers to take the keep."

"Are you sure?" Val asked.

Galin nodded.

"Do you agree with the boy?" Val asked Brock.

Brock took a swig of ale. "Yeah, actually, I do." He looked right at Val. "We can do this."

"What's this place called?" Galin asked.

Brock smiled. "Iron Fist Keep."

The man at the next table got up and left the tavern.

"Galin! Galin, come quickly!" Ellis yelled as he ran across the tavern. "Keya did it."

Galin leaped to his feet. "Jena's cured?"

Ellis nodded. "Come on."

Galin ran after Ellis towards their room.

THE MUSCULAR, blond-haired man with blue eyes walked towards a large, one-story building across town. Unlike the rest of the village, this building was elaborate and well kept. A large man stood guard outside the double doors. As he got closer, his form blurred. His ears became pointed and his skin became blue. The blond hair turned black. Tasar's thin lips smiled at the man as he pulled out his spell components pouch. He reached inside and pulled out an eye from a newt. "Lia fol penia," Tasar said. "Lia fol penia. Lia fol penia." He clutched his eyes as the sharp pain pierced the back of his eyes.

"I can't see!" the guard said as he clutched his eyes, falling to the ground. "I'm blind!"

Tasar blinked as the pain receded. "I love that spell." He kicked the sobbing man as he pushed his way through the double doors. Inside was a large, open room with the walls lined with chests, crates, and piles of loot from the townspeople. There was no furniture in the room, only a pathway to the back. His head moved side to side, looking for more guards. Nothing. Nothing, except for the light coming through the cracked door at the back of the room. Tasar smiled as he stepped towards the door.

"What do you want?" Brice demanded as Tasar flung the door open. "My guard should have told you that I'm not available right now."

Tasar grinned at the slightly overweight but strong brown-eyed man. Unlike the others in town, Brice's long, brown hair was well groomed. His clothes were clean and flamboyant. "I see you don't work the farm too much."

"I already paid this month," Brice said as he sat back down at his wooden desk with a ledger book on top. He continued updating his inventory as he said, "Please leave me be."

"Who do you think I am?" Tasar asked.

Brice glared at him. "Do you think I'm stupid? You're with the Darkstriders. Your taxes are worse than Kade's."

"I'm not with the Darkstriders," Tasar said.

"Orc crap. You're a Dark Elf, aren't you?" Brice asked.

"Yes."

"Then, you're with them. Now go away or I'll have my guard toss you out on your backside," Brice said.

Tasar's thin lips curled. "He's having trouble seeing right now."

"What did you do to Larry?" Brice demanded.

"I blinded him. Don't worry, it's not permanent." Tasar waved his hand by Brice face. "I'm here to help you."

Brice cocked his head. "Help me? Why?"

"We have a mutual enemy, Prince Galin V of Ravenward," Tasar said. "He came into your town to recruit your people to join his cause."

Brice laughed. "We saw one of them trying a few days ago. That old man is not a threat."

Tasar began to pace around the room. "They are going to kill you."

Brice blinked. "Who?"

"The prince," Tasar replied. "I'll help you kill them."

Brice smiled. "So, you need *my help*?" He leaned back in his chair. "What's in it for me?"

Tasar's face hardened. "You stay alive." His face twitched. "I believe the governor, Artis the Black, would be very, very grateful to you."

Brice raised an eyebrow. "Really? Why would he care?"

"Well, he hired me to kill the boy, but not to make a martyr out of him," Tasar said. "If it looks like someone besides the Darkstriders did it, he won't be a martyr and that ridiculous prophecy will finally be forgotten."

"You're an...assassin?"

"Of sorts," Tasar said. "I consider myself more of an independent contractor."

Brice shook his head. "No way. I don't get involved in Darkstrider business and they don't get involved in mine. I won't help you."

Tasar looked down at the ring on Brice's finger. "Are you married?"

"Yeah, so?"

Tasar rubbed his chin. "If you won't help me, maybe I'll have to give her to the Feral Orcs. They love to take human females for pleasure." He grinned. "But, the females usually don't survive it."

Brice jumped out of his chair and glared at Tasar. "Don't threaten my family!"

"I was just adding some leverage to our...negotiations," Tasar said. "However, they do have women among them. You could have them all."

Brice frowned. "What would I do with them?"

Tasar leaned up against the wall. "I don't know, how about selling them to the orcs at the checkpoint to the north? They'd pay a lot for that kind of...entertainment. What do you think?" Tasar extended his hand to Brice.

Brice shook Tasar's hand. "What's the plan?"

Tasar smiled.

GALIN BURST INTO THE ROOM. Jena was still covered with sweat, but her eyes were open. "Jena!"

Keya got up off the floor. "Just a few minutes, she needs to rest."

Galin watched Keya close the door behind her. He knelt down next to Jena. "How do you feel?"

Jena glared at him. "How do you think I feel?" She blinked as if willing away her feelings. "I'm sorry. Mother said that I'll be irritable for a few days."

He wiped the sweat from her forehead. "It's okay. I'll still be here."

Her pleading eyes tugged at his heart. "Galin, I want to get married today. No, right now. I don't want die without being with you first."

Galin shook his head. "We just figured out how to bring the fighters in hiding to join us, but we have to take Iron Fist Keep."

"What does that have to do with us getting married?" Jena demanded.

"I think we need to wait," Galin said.

Jena tore her eyes away from him. "You don't love me anymore, do you?"

Galin's heart sank into his boots. "Of course I love you. But, I want a great wedding." He swallowed. "Maybe, we could get married at Iron Fist Keep, after we take it."

Jena rolled her head towards him. "Okay, but this is your last chance. You asked me, remember?"

Galin held up his hands. "I promise. No more delays. We'll be married on the first piece of liberated territory." He smiled. "Can you get any more romantic than that?" He kissed her forehead.

"I love you," Jena said.

"I love you, too." Galin headed for the door. "Get some sleep." *As if I needed another thing to worry about,* he thought as he left the room.

CHAPTER 11

All About Keya

A few hours later, Galin and Ellis were sitting at a round table in the middle of the Cowardly Owl. The room was nearly empty, even though it was dinnertime. *Maybe people don't eat out here,* Galin thought. The sweet aroma of roasting rabbit made his stomach growl in anticipation.

A young beer wench put two ales on the table. "Here you go," she said. "Your dinner will be ready soon."

Galin nodded. "Thank you." He snickered at Ellis, who was practically drooling over her as she walked away. "Can you be any more obvious?"

"Hey, you've got female company, I don't. I need some," Ellis said.

Galin looked across the table at him and smiled. "I

want to thank you for helping me save Jena. I can never repay you for what you did. Thank you."

Ellis waved him off. "Knock that crap off or I'll kick your ass. We're friends and I'm always with you and that's that." He looked away. "But, if you wanted to buy the next round, I wouldn't stop you."

"Sure, why not?" Galin asked. He looked up as three large men with swords and a Dark Elf in a dark robe burst through the door.

The bartender rushed to the front. "Hey, you can't do that."

The large man with brown hair smacked him in the throat.

The bartender fell to floor, gasping for air.

Galin and Ellis leaped to their feet, drawing their weapons.

The beer wench bolted upstairs.

Tasar pointed at Galin and Ellis. "Over there, Jack."

Jack motioned to the others. "Lee, go to the right. Bill, go to the left."

"They're just kids!" Lee protested. "This isn't right."

Jack glared at him. "Just do it and shut up."

Galin, with his sword drawn, sidestepped away from the table. "Who are you?" he asked Tasar.

Ellis was whirling daggers as he stepped towards Lee. "You should be afraid of us."

"You don't want to do this," Galin said. "The beer wench ran to get help."

Jack laughed. "These cretins? They won't dare lift a finger against Brice." His face reddened. "Get them!"

Bill charged at Ellis.

Ellis leaped off to the side and dropped to the ground. He swung his left leg at Lee's feet, knocking him on the ground.

Jack raised his sword and swung at Galin.

Lee charged at Galin from the side.

In one fluid motion, Galin blocked Jack's sword and swung at Lee's mid-section.

Ellis pounced on Bill like a lion and slammed both daggers into his eyes. As he ripped them from Bill's skull, blood gushed from his eyes sockets.

Lee collapsed to the ground as his intestines spilled out onto the floor.

"Galin!" a female voice yelled from across the room, running down the stairs.

Tasar frowned.

Jack swept Galin's leg, slamming him to the floor.

Tasar pulled out a cedar chip, holding it in his left hand. "Sky din jivla bron."

"Watch out!" Keya yelled as she ran towards them.

Ellis looked up.

Jack moved away to face her.

"Sky din jivla bron," Tasar said. The small cedar chip burst into six balls of flame, hovering just above Tasar's palm.

Galin swung at Jack.

Jack knocked it away and moved back to Tasar.

"Sky din jivla bron," Tasar said. The six fire bolts launched towards Galin.

Galin swallowed. It was too late to call up his defensive magic. He closed his eyes, waiting for death to come.

Keya pushed Galin out of the way.

All six bolts hit Keya in the chest, melting her flesh and bone.

"No!" Brock yelled as he charged at Jack with his sword raised.

Jack easily batted Brock's slash away. "Time to go."

"I'm already gone." Tasar rubbed his hand as he ran out the door, with Jack close behind.

Brock dropped his sword and knelt down, holding Keya's head in his lap. Tears poured down his cheeks. "She's gone. No, not her, too." He stared at the sky. "Why? By the gods, why do you hate me so much?"

Two local men rushed inside the tavern. The larger started to open his mouth, until he saw Keya lying on the floor.

"Mother!" Jena yelled. She ran over to Brock. Her eyes fell as she saw that Keya no longer had a chest. "I can't heal that." She hugged her mother. "I'm sorry, I'm so sorry, Mother."

Ellis tapped Galin on the shoulder. "We've got to get those guys before they bring back some more friends."

"We know where Brice's warehouse is. Maybe they went there," said the local man with long, brown hair. "I'm Brent, and this is Steve," he said, pointing at the other man with braided black hair. "We'll show you if you want."

Galin looked at Brock. "Will you come with us?"

Brock rose to his feet. "I will."

"Right." Galin led the others out onto the street.

～

Brent led them to the other side of the village. Peering around a corner of a house, so as not to be seen, he pointed to the one-story building ahead of them. "That's it."

Galin moved forward to get a good look. The sun was falling asleep over the horizon. The one-story building had large wooden double doors. Unlike all the other buildings in the village, it was well kept. It almost looked out of place. There were three men armed with hand axes just outside the double doors. He slid back out of sight and moved over to the others. "Brent, Steve, thank you for showing us. You can go if you want to."

Brent shook his said. "No, we'll stay."

Galin nodded. "Okay."

"How do we deal with that Dark Elf?" Ellis asked. "You saw what he did to Keya."

Galin looked up at Brock. "Father?"

Brock frowned. "The spell he cast was something Beldroth used during battles against the Darkstriders."

"She was on our side then?" Ellis asked.

"No, she wasn't. She was a Dark Elf pyromancer. She'd make the sky rain fire and opened up a hole in the walls of Staerdale Castle," Brock said. "She was devoted to Kade the Usurper. She was as cunning and sly as they come."

Galin rubbed his chin. "Maybe he's a pyromancer, too? I saw some of them being trained at Tadus School of Magic."

"How do we fight him? None of us are wizards," Brent said.

Galin glared at him. "No one said you had to stay." He smiled at Ellis. "I'll follow Nyna's good advice. Let's go."

Brock drew his sword. "For Keya."

Galin and the others nodded. "Spread out as we get closer to them. We don't them to get more help," Galin said. He swallowed. It was darker than just a few moments ago. That helped. He willed visions of Jena being captured and attacked by the Dark Elf. A small tingle spread throughout his body from his heart. He emerged from around the corner of the small house, facing the three men. Like a flock of birds flying in formation, Brock and Ellis slid to his right and Brent and Steve moved to his left, not in a line, but an arrowhead. "Follow me!" Galin yelled as he charged at the three men.

When the guards looked up, fear fell over their faces like a mask. They ran inside and slammed the door shut behind them.

Galin pointed around the corner. "Brent, Steve, see if there is another way in."

"You got it," Brent said as they bolted around the corner.

Galin yanked on the door handle. It didn't budge. "Bar?"

"Let me see," Ellis said as he pushed his way through. He peered through the crack between the door. "Nope, there's no bar." He grasped the door handle. "It's locked. Give me a second." He pulled out a small leather case from his pants pocket.

Brock glared at him as Ellis unclipped the case. "What is that?"

Ellis shrugged. "Just something to help me get into places." He pulled out two thin iron lock picks. "I'll have this open in a minute."

"Where'd you learn this?" Brock demanded. "Your father was a baker."

Ellis smiled. "He was a lousy baker." His tongue hung out the corner of his mouth as he worked on the lock.

Brent and Steve emerged from behind the building. "No other way out. No doors or windows."

"Strange," Galin said.

Brent shrugged.

Click.

"I got it," Ellis said. He slid his pouch back into his pants and drew his daggers.

Brock put his hand on Galin's shoulder. "It's a trap."

Galin looked into Brock's eyes. "I know." With his free hand, he flung the door open. Tiny arcs began dancing across his skin. Galin's eyes began to glow. The arcs jumped from his hands and made his sword glow. *Think defense*, Galin thought. *Think defense.*

Brock and Ellis moved in behind him and Brent and Steve close by.

Galin looked around. The walls were lined with chests and piles of tribute the local people were forced to give to Brice. If he defended this place, he'd have a million places to hide. His stomach danced as he moved forward. Where were they? Galin was more than a quarter of the way through the room and . . . nothing. Did the pyromancer make a magic tunnel to somewhere else? Galin whirled around as the doors slammed behind them.

"Get them!" Brice yelled from the back room.

Steve and Brent charged the two men that slammed the door.

Galin stared right at Tasar, who was standing in the doorway across the room. Six men came out from behind the piles of loot, armed with short swords. "I've got the Dark Elf."

Ellis rolled his eyes. "Of course, you only have to take one bad guy, sire."

Tasar held out a cedar chip. His lips were moving as if casting a spell.

Think defense, Galin thought. With his glowing sword raised, he charged at Tasar.

Six fire bolts flew across the room right at Galin.

Defense! Galin's rage grew as images of his dead adoptive mother flashed through his mind.

The fire bolts bounced off Galin's skin, hitting two guards.

They collapsed to the ground as their skin began to dissolve.

Tasar blinked and disappeared into the back room.

Two guards lunged at Ellis.

"You don't want to fight me," Ellis said as he side-stepped their blows. "I mean, it's not fair to you." He whipped one dagger at the large man. It found its mark and the man dropped to the ground.

The other swung his short sword at Ellis, cutting into his right leg.

Brock charged at two guards with his long sword at the ready.

They stepped back as Brock swung his sword.

Brock recovered. He thrust his sword straight in the chest of the guard on the right. Brock lost his grip as he tried to yank it out from the man's chest.

The other guard swung his sword at Brock.

Brock grabbed the guard that he had just killed and spun him around and ducked.

The guard decapitated the dead guard.

As Ellis fell to the ground, he flung his last dagger at the guard. The dagger embedded itself into the man's throat. He scrambled to pull his weapons from his victims.

Brock slammed the headless guard into the other one, and his sword skewered them both. After he watched the life leave the guard's eyes, he pulled his sword from their gullets.

Steve screamed.

"Help us!" Brent screamed before he lost his head.

Offense, think offense, Galin thought as he charged the last two guards. His skin and his eyes were still glowing.

The two guards dropped their swords and ran out the door, slamming it behind them.

Galin whirled around. "Now for the Dark Elf." He raced towards the back room with Brock right behind him and Ellis limping along.

The back room had a large wooden desk in the middle with an empty chair behind it. Brice was cowering in the corner as Galin entered the room with his eyes still glowing. "Where is he? Where's the Dark Elf?" Galin demanded.

Brice tried to push himself further into the corner as Galin approached. "He's gone."

"How?" Galin demanded.

Brice's face was ghostly white. "A light. He cast a spell and…and he vanished."

"You are responsible for Keya's death!" Brock yelled. He raised his sword. "If I can't get the Dark Elf, I'll take your head instead."

Brice held up his hands, pressing himself closer to the floor. "Please, please no. I beg of you."

Galin closed his eyes as he sheathed his sword. He willed the dragon magic away. His eyes flashed open. "Who was it? Why did you come after us?"

Warm fluid seeped through Brice's trousers. "He said he'd give my wife to the Feral Orcs."

"Who?" Galin demanded.

"Tasar, his name is Tasar. He was hired by Artis the Black to kill you," Brice said. "He had to do it in such a way that you wouldn't be a martyr."

Ellis blinked. "Why?"

"If Galin becomes a martyr, he'll be the rallying cry for every warrior in Axain," Brock said. "They would never be able to stop all of them and they know it."

"Who's Artis the Black?" Galin asked.

"The governor," Brock said. "He rules over the Darkstrider territory east of the Wailing Mountains."

"I've told you everything," Brice said. "Please, have mercy."

Galin nodded. "I—"

Brock raised his sword. "You'll get the same mercy that Keya got." He brought it down like an ax, severing Brice's head in two. He chopped Brice again and again and again.

"Stop!" Galin yelled as he pushed Brock out of the tiny room. "Stop, it's over."

Tears flowed down Brock's face. "I didn't tell you; we were going to be married. I was going to tell you, but I didn't have a chance." He shook his head. "Now, I've lost both of them."

Ellis limped out of the back room. "Damn, I hope you don't get pissed at me."

"Come on, let's go," Galin said as he rushed back to Jena. Would she be as vengeful about losing her mother as he was about losing his?

CHAPTER 12

Grieving

As soon as Galin got back to the Cowardly Owl, he rushed inside. Tables were overturned and the stools were thrown about. His eyes zeroed in on Jena sobbing over Keya's body. He knelt down next to her. "I'm sorry. I didn't mean for this to happen."

Jena looked up at him. Her eyes were red and puffy. "It's not your fault." Her face turned as dark as the lich they fought in the Infernal Grotto. "It's that damned Dark Elf! I'll kill him." She leaped to her feet, grabbed a stool and hurled it across the room. She collapsed to the floor. "I couldn't heal her." She shook her head as tears flowed down her cheeks like a rushing river. "I…I tried…I tried over and over and over again, Galin. It didn't work."

He pulled her in close. "It's all right, my love." His heart faltered as he felt rage emanate from her body.

"Jena!" Brock yelled as he carried Ellis inside. "He's hurt."

"Not him too!" Jena rushed over to Ellis as Brock laid him down on the floor. She pulled out an incense ball from her spell component pouch as she knelt down next to him. "He's lost a lot of blood."

"Is it too late?" Brock asked.

Jena shook her head. "No, this is too easy." She placed the incense into a small dragon-shaped silver incense bowl. The smoke had a slight green tint as it rose into the air. Jena placed her hand on Ellis' wounded leg. She closed her eyes and put her hands together in prayer. "Min touch Helbred nom." Jena's body began to sway back and forth. "Min touch Helbred nom."

Ellis' leg began to twitch.

"Min touch Helbred nom." A laceration ripped through Jena's leg.

The wound on Ellis' leg closed up. He smiled as he sat up.

Jena screamed. Blood poured from her leg, spilling out onto the floor.

"Jena!" Galin screamed as he reached for her.

Brock snatched him backwards. "Leave her be. This is normal, remember?"

Galin nodded.

Jena bit her lip. She sat on the floor and bowed her head. Her mouth moved as if whispering a plea to the goddess Odella herself. After a moment, her leg began to glow. The gushing blood slowed to a trickle, then it stopped altogether. Her gaping wound closed. She opened her eyes. "I'm okay, Galin." She looked over at her mother. "I'll need help burying her."

Brock stood up. "I'll help you."

"Me too," Galin said.

Brock picked up Keya and headed out the door.

A FEW HOURS LATER, Galin and Jena returned to their room. They were sitting on the bed next to one another, holding hands. He looked into her eyes. What if that was Jena and not her mother? Could they really wait until they took Iron Fist Keep? That could be years, or maybe never. No, she was right before. It was time that he did what he'd asked her to do nearly two years ago. "I was thinking about us—"

"You were right," Jena said as she tore her eyes away. "We need to wait."

Was this karma? Galin shook his head. "No, I don't want to wait. You were right. If we wait too long, we'll never get married. I asked you, remember?"

Jena nodded. "I know, but this changes things. I understand now; how you must have felt after your mother was murdered by...them." Her face hardened. "Nothing is more important to me than getting that thing that killed my mother. I don't want our marriage tainted with this...hatred."

Galin swallowed as he saw his loving Jena turn into a vengeful monster. Was that his doing? He shook his head. "I want to get married now, before I lose you."

Her eyes bore into him like a wild dog's teeth tears at its prey. "No."

His pleading eyes fell as her face became stern. "Don't let it consume you, as it did me."

"I won't," she said.

Galin looked away. *What have I done?*

A FEW MILES east of Nia, along the base of the Wailing Mountains, a bright light appeared just above the ground and Tasar stepped out of it. As soon as he exited the portal, it disappeared. His steed was still tied off to a tree on the outskirts of his camp. The camp was in a clearing of nearly impassable underbrush. It was not a natural clearing, but one that he'd burnt into the soul of the countryside.

Tasar kicked the cold fire pit. "How did he survive? It's simply not possible! No human could have done that." He closed his eyes and took a breath. *Could he really be the one? What if the Darkstrider's were correct? They were fools, but occasionally they were right.* He sat down next to the fire pit. Tasar waved his hand over the fire pit and a tiny fire started in the center.

He looked towards the town. Sure, when he took the job he didn't believe that Galin was the prophesied boy king. What sane Dark Elf would? The prophecy claimed that a human boy king that can wield magic would unite the world against the Dark Elves and destroy them. Tasar snorted. The prophecy was written generations ago. But, what if he was the one?

Others would follow him simply because the foolish Darkstriders fear him.

Tasar pulled out a water skin and took a sip. Maybe it was too late to avoid the effect that making him a martyr would cause. Perhaps? If he was thought of as a martyr, people would rally behind him; not all, but a good number. The real question was how many would rally behind a *prophesied king* that makes the Darkstriders quiver in their boots? Tasar frowned. Probably, a lot more. No more games.

How should he fight Galin, especially since his fire bolts bounced right off him? Every mage has defensive spells, why not Galin? Tasar didn't see spell components in Galin's hand or him even whispering an incantation, which was consistent with the prophecy. But, he still had to call up his power, right? Yeah, that had to be right. If he surprised him, then he could win. No different than if he was battling another mage.

Perhaps he could profit even more from this... encounter, maybe. The Darkstriders always paid handsomely for intelligence on uprisings. Imagine what they would pay to know about the uprising that the prophesied boy king was starting? Tasar's lips stretched across his face. He would have to get a cart to carry all the crowns they would pay him and he'd still get paid by Artis the Black. No more holding back, no more. It was time for Galin to see Tasar's real power.

CHAPTER 13

Galin's Army

Brock, Ellis, Galin, and Jena were walking through the cornfields a few miles west of Nia. "It's just a little further," Brock said. "The farmer is too old join us, but he gave us a place to train our volunteers."

Galin blinked as they emerged into an opening in the rows of corn. It was huge. There were pine and oak trees to the south, but cornrows protected the clearing from prying eyes. "Why is this area not planted?"

"He said that this field is for his winter crops," Brock replied as he headed towards the wood line. "There's supposed to be a stream out here, too. We'll need a water supply."

Galin nodded.

Jena, *not* holding Galin's hand, asked, "Why won't they find us here?"

Ellis blinked. "Are you dumb? We just walked through a corn jungle that is bigger than my father's ass. Unless they follow *you* here, we're good."

Jena scowled at him.

"Knock it off, you two," Galin said. His eyes sagged as he watched his beloved Jena turn into something... else. What had he done? Maybe she wouldn't be like this if he'd married her like he promised long ago. Maybe . . .

"There it is," Brock said, pointing at the rushing water thirty feet inside the woods. "It's a good size, too."

"Is it enough?" Galin asked.

Brock nodded. "Yeah, I think so."

Galin looked back at the clearing. "Is that big enough to train everyone? Even the new volunteers from Nia?"

"How many are coming from Nia?" Jena asked.

Brock smiled. "Since Brice was killed, they're coming out in droves. I was told that word got as far south as Plaka and Grurg."

Galin turned to Ellis and Jena. "Can you give me and my father a moment?"

"Sure," Jena said as she led Ellis away.

"What is it?" Brock asked. The concern on his face could not be missed.

Galin swallowed. "I don't know if I can do this." He sat down next to an oak tree by the stream. "I mean, I know nothing about military planning or taking a keep or anything like that." His insides churned as his pleading eyes looked up at Brock. "I'm in way over my head."

Brock sat down next to his adopted son. "You're right."

"What?"

"You're not educated in military strategy and tactics. You never even trained anyone to do anything, ever," Brock said. He smiled. "But, I'll follow you. You see, good leaders can think on their feet and usually know the right things to do, but great leaders listen to those who've been trained and have experience. I don't mean you'd have to do everything they say, but you must listen. The first step into greatness is to know your own weaknesses. Once you know that, you'll know what strengths to look for when assembling your advisers."

"Advisers? What advisers?" Galin asked.

"You'll have them soon enough," Brock said. Galin felt Brock's soft eyes looking right into his soul. "Your real job is to inspire others to greatness. Everyone can do much more than they believe." Brock pointed at Galin's chest.

Galin looked away. "People will die because of me, like before."

"No, not like before," Brock said. "Before, people sacrificed themselves to give you a chance. Now, when people die in battle, they are not dying for you, but to give their families a chance at freedom." He got up. "Your greatest enemy is yourself. Don't let it defeat you before the war even begins." Brock walked towards Ellis and Jena.

Galin tossed a small rock into the stream. What was he supposed to do? Advisers? Chance at freedom? He looked back at the others. They all believed in him. Why? Being able to use dragon magic was no reason to follow someone. Maybe that was why the warriors still in hiding wanted to see a victory first before they would commit. Did he blame them? No, not at all. He had to try, otherwise Sally and Keya would have died for nothing. How could he, a young man, inspire would-be warriors? Did he have to defeat someone in a contest? Did he have to outsmart another in a debate? Did he have to tell stories about his adventures? No, none of those would work. If Galin wouldn't be inspired by those things, why should they? Galin stared at the rushing water. *Think, come on, think.*

Hours later, Galin, Jena, Brock, and Ellis were sitting next to the fire in the center of the clearing. His head turned as the cornstalks rustled. He stood up. He smiled as the volunteers began to pour onto the open field, men and women carrying swords and packs. Three carts carrying supplies plowed their way through the cornfield. He smiled.

Brock directed the volunteers to stand in a semi-military formation, as if the training had already started.

"How many are there?" Jena asked as she watched the volunteers continue to pour into the clearing.

Galin shook his head. "Not sure."

Ellis grinned. "I'd bet at least five hundred." He slapped Galin on the back. "You've got a real army now."

"Yeah, I do," Galin sighed. He never really believed that he'd ever get this far, let alone lead an army. Was it enough to take Iron Fist Keep? Were they trained at all? Or was this the first time they had ever carried a sword? Too often, peasants were threatened and only fought out of fear, not loyalty. If he ever became king, he'd never do that. But, how would the people know what kind of ruler he would be? It was perfectly acceptable to abuse the troops in the name of military training, but would that really improve their chances against a battle-hardened Feral Orc regiment? No, not likely. If someone was fighting for a cause they truly believed in, they should fight harder, right? Galin would, why wouldn't they?

Brock walked over to Galin. "They're ready for inspection."

"Inspection?" Galin whispered. "What am I supposed to do?"

Brock leaned in close. "Just walk up and down the line and shake a few hands. Thank them for coming, etcetera."

Galin swallowed.

"You can do it," Brock said. "I believe in you."

Galin straightened up. "Okay." The volunteers were lined up in ten rows and they extended from one end of the clearing to the other. Galin walked up and down each line, shaking every hand until his hands hurt. He looked into their eyes and saw one thing; fear. It was rampant throughout the ranks like a disease. Did he blame them? No, he was afraid, too. He was going to ask them to do things that would get some, if not all of them, killed. Volunteering before the first battle was one thing, staying with it after the fight was another.

Brock said his real job was to inspire them. With all his doubts, how could he? He'd lost his adoptive mother and Keya, and nearly lost Jena. How could he lead these people to victory over the Darkstriders? He looked over at Brock. His adoptive father had the most experience in warfare than anyone else here; perhaps he should lead them? Galin and Brock walked to the front of the formation. "How many do we have?"

"Five hundred seventy-four," Brock said. "All of them are farmers or simple peasants. No trained warriors among them."

"They look very scared," Galin whispered.

Brock nodded. "They are."

Galin bit his lip. If he told them to go home now, everyone who gave their lives to make this day happen would have died in vain, including Sally. His stomach wrenched and twisted. Images of Sally ran through his mind. Especially they day he found her murdered in their own home. He shivered at the torture she must have endured to protect him. No, they wouldn't die for nothing.

Galin climbed up on top of a cart and looked at the formation.

"What are you doing?" Brock demanded.

Ignoring him, Galin motioned to the volunteers. "I want everyone to come closer so you can hear me." A smile crept across his face as they encircled the wagon.

"What are you going to say?" Brock asked.

Galin swallowed. What indeed? Should he have thought about that *before* he called them over? Too late now. His throat dried up. Galin smiled at the crowd staring up at him. "Today marks the beginning of the great journey to restore the kingdom of Axain from the clutches of the Darkstriders. Many people died to make this day possible. It started with the first and only female knight in the kingdom, Thea the Loyal, who enabled my adoptive parents to save me from the clutches of the Darkstriders. Death has continued to follow my new family until this very day. But, we have a few things on our side that gives us the upper hand."

"One, they fear me because of an ancient Dark Elf prophecy. I am the only human male that I know of who can wield magic. Not just any magic, but dragon magic," Galin said. "Two, no one is forcing anyone to fight. You fight for freedom, not because of coercion, like our enemy."

"If I was sitting where you are, I'd be wondering one thing. When Galin V becomes king, how will it be different?" Galin paused as he stared out at the crowd. Where was he going with this? "One thing I wish we had was the people represented in the King's Court. You will have a voice in my government. You'll be able to speak your mind when you agree or disagree, as long as it is not violent. That is freedom. May your grandchildren never know the horrors of this day."

"I'm going to tell you the truth. It will be a very long journey, and not all of us will make it back," Galin said. "But when we win the war and kick those Darkstriders back across the Fadyhl Waters, everyone who died since the day of my birth will not have died in vain. Rather, they will have helped forge a path towards... victory!" Galin said as he threw both hands in the air.

The crowd cheered.

A tear ran down Brock's cheek. "That's my boy."

Ellis and Jena both clapped.

Galin smiled. *We can do this.*

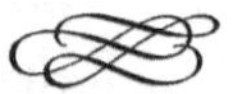

CHAPTER 14

Infiltrated

In less than three weeks, the rebel camp was bustling. Tents filled the southern half of the clearing. Galin and Jena's tent was right next to the fire pit. Next to it was the largest tent in the camp, Jena's hospital tent. Rows upon rows of swords, shields, quivers, arrows, and bows ran in between all the tents, as if to use every possible inch of the clearing.

Galin walked through the tents, past the weapons and into the open. The volunteers were divided up into groups. The eastern section was lined with targets along the edge of the cornfield. The volunteers were in formation with bows drawn.

"Fire!" Ellis commanded.

They released their bows. Some of the arrows

plunged into their targets and others were lost in the cornfield.

Galin smiled. He never saw Ellis happier. Another group were paired off with one volunteer lying on the ground. The other was practicing to put on a battle dressing, with Jena checking each one. True, Jena could easily heal most wounds, but they needed to be alive until she could get to them, hence the bandages. At the very least, it would give the volunteers some comfort when Jena was not around. Galin frowned. They needed more Priestesses of Odella. But where could they find some that would join their cause?

The clanging of dueling sticks tore Galin's gaze to the western section of the clearing. As if practicing for some glorious epic battle, around two hundred volunteers were sparring with stick swords. Brock was walking up and down the lines like a drill sergeant, correcting blows and fighting stances.

As soon as Brock saw Galin, he walked over to his adopted son. "Want to join in?"

Galin shook his head. "Not today. I'm still sore from our little brawl yesterday," he said, rubbing his right shoulder. "This reminds me of us sparring behind the house."

Brock smiled. "I guess it does." His smiled disappeared. "We can't delay too much longer."

Galin cocked his head. "What's the rush? I thought the warriors were waiting for a victory from us. I'm sure they'll understand that we have to prepare first."

"They may not. Besides, the longer we stay here, the more likely the Darkstriders will find us," Brock said.

Galin looked upon the sparring masses. "Are they ready?"

Brock shook his head. "No. I don't think so."

Galin glared at him. "Then how can we go now? It would be like sending a flock of sheep alone to the wolves!"

"No, it doesn't work that way," Brock said. "No one is ever truly ready for combat. Besides, we have a smaller target that we can hit first. Actually, we have to hit it because of the amount of volunteers we have."

"What are you suggesting?" Galin asked.

"Iron Fist Keep is on the far side of the Wailing Mountains. To get to the mountains, we have to take out the checkpoint," Brock said. "Once we are in the mountains, we can hide our forces while we figure out how to take the keep."

Galin sniffed. "You make it sound so easy."

"It's not. We need to send a reconnaissance patrol to the checkpoint to see exactly what is there. What do you think?" Brock asked.

"Do we have a choice?"

Brock shook his head. "No, not really."

"That's what I thought. I'm going to get a drink." Galin headed towards the stream.

JUST INSIDE THE WOOD LINE, the stream made him smile. Galin knelt down over the rushing water. He scooped up the clear water in his hands and slurped it down. Nothing tasted better than clean, fresh water.

His ears perked. Someone was coming. Galin looked through the few trees towards the tents.

A muscular man with long, blond hair pulled back into a ponytail carrying a short sword rushed towards him.

"What are you doing?" Galin asked.

The man said nothing.

Galin reached for his sword as he stood up.

The man knocked his sword to the ground. Within half a heartbeat, he thrust his sword through Galin's belly. The man smiled as his form became blurred. His long, blond hair became black. His blue eyes sunk into black, lifeless eyes. The fair skin transformed into a deep blue. "I should have done this in the first place," Tasar said. "You may not need spell components or incantations, but you do need time."

Pain. The pain raced throughout his body. Galin winced. "You'll pay for this."

Tasar smiled. "I don't think so. I'm just going to collect your head and be on my way." He raised his short sword.

Galin closed his eyes. He was truly a failure, there was no getting around it now. Maybe everyone would be better off if he was dead.

"Galin!" Brock yelled as he bolted towards Tasar with his sword drawn.

Galin's eyes flashed open. "I'm not giving up that easy." He rolled away as Tasar's sword hit the ground.

"Intruder!" Brock yelled. "By the river!"

Tasar looked back at Brock, who was a mere few yards away. He bolted into the woods.

Brock stood over Galin, staring into the woods. "He…disappeared." He knelt down over Galin. Blood was pouring out of his stomach. Brock bit his lip as he pulled up his shirt. "It's deep, but at least he didn't slash there. Otherwise your innards would be all over the ground."

Spots. Cold. "It's fatal. I know it is," Galin said. "I'm so sorry. I failed you."

"You forget, we have a healer with us. I've seen them heal worse." Brock smiled. "You don't get off that easy."

Six volunteers arrived with swords in their hands. "Where are they?" one of them asked.

Brock shook his head. "Too late now. Let's get him to the medical tent."

Galin grimaced as they helped him to his feet. "Let's get you to Jena."

"Okay," Galin said.

They helped Galin to the medical tent.

THE LARGE TENT had eight tables set up and Jena was instructing three nurses on triaging patients when Galin was rushed inside.

"Cold," Galin said. "I feel so cold."

"No! Not him, too!" Jena yelled as she ran to his side.

Brock hurried the others out of the tent and closed the flap. "What can I do?"

"He's lost a lot of blood," Jena said. "There's only one thing we can do." Her tearful eyes looked right at

Brock. "Don't let me hit the floor after I heal him. Okay?"

"Sure," Brock said as he moved next to Jena.

Galin looked at Jena and smiled. "I love you. I'm so sorry."

She put her finger over his lips. "Shh. Be still." Jena wiped the tears from her eyes. "Could you pass me that small bowl on the table over there?"

"Sure," Brock said.

Galin's forehead glistened with sweat. "I should have married you already."

Jena smiled. "Stop talking like you're dying. I can cast Odella's touch three times a day, and you're in luck."

"Is that why you still use bandages?" Brock asked as he gave her the small incense bowl.

Jena nodded. "Yes." She poured some incense into the bowl, lit it, and placed it next to Galin's head. She put her hands together as if praying to the goddess Odella. After a moment, she placed her hands on Galin's abdomen. "Min touch Helbred nom."

Warmth fell over Galin like a blanket. His wound began to glow.

"Min touch Helbred nom," Jena said.

The pain began to leave Galin. All the cold and fearful feelings left with the pain. He felt his wound closing.

Jena winced as if she'd been stabbed by an invisible sword. "Min touch Helbred nom." Jena keeled over in pain.

Brock caught her as she fell. He laid her gently on the ground.

"I...I feel good," Galin said. He sat up and his mouth dropped as he saw his Jena covered in blood. Galin couldn't take his eyes off the growing pool of blood around her. "Father?"

Jena, as if in her own world, sat up and placed her hands together in prayer. Her mouth moved, but nothing audible came out. After a moment, her torso glowed a bright white, just for a second, then it was gone. Her eyes opened and she smiled. "I hate that part," Jena said as she stood up. Her soft eyes looked right into Galin's soul. "How do you feel?"

"I'm fine. I worry about you," Galin said.

Jena looked down at her bloody tunic and smiled. "There goes another one."

Brock rubbed his chin. "I didn't know that you could only heal three times a day."

Jena nodded. "That's why we have to triage patients and only the worst ones that can be healed will be healed. We'll use more conventional methods for the others." She looked right at Galin. "I'll always heal you, no matter what the cost. I won't lose you, too."

Galin swallowed. He held her hand. "You won't. I love you."

Jena leaned over and kissed him. "I love you, too."

"I'll leave you two alone," Brock said as he started for the door.

"What happened?" Jena asked.

Brock stopped and turned around. "That Dark Elf attacked Galin."

"Yeah, he caught me by surprise. He was in human form. I've seen him around. He must have come in a few weeks ago with the volunteers," Galin said. He looked up at Brock. "Think there's more of them?"

Brock came closer to Galin. "Probably."

"He did you detect them before? When you were at Staerdale Castle?" Jena asked.

"We didn't," Brock replied. "They infiltrated the castle, the King's Court, and some were even knights." Brock tore his eyes away from his adopted son. "Like humans, only a few of them use magic, and magic comes at a cost to anyone who casts it. Well, that was what Beldroth used to say. What do we do?"

Jena shrugged and looked to Galin.

Galin sighed. What did they expect from him? Sure, he gave a speech, so what? Galin bit his lip. If they stayed until they were a well-trained unit, the Darkstriders would certainly come in and wipe them out. What if they moved the camp to another location? No, the resistance was waiting for some kind of victory and they wouldn't wait too long, right? It would be his responsibility if he sent his new army into a fight they couldn't win. He would be the one making widows and orphans, not the Darkstriders. Why were they stupid enough to follow him, anyway? If they were caught or lost the war, all those people who died to protect him would have died for nothing. He loved Sally, his adoptive mother, and Keya. He couldn't—no, he wouldn't—let them die for nothing. No, no way. His chest puffed out as a wave of confidence swept through his body. "We've got to hit them now."

"They're not ready," Brock said.

"We need more healers," Jena protested.

Galin shook his head. "We don't have the time. That Dark Elf was probably Tasar, the one Brice told us about. The assassin hired by Artis the Black." His hardened eyes looked right at Brock. "If you were him, what would you do?"

"I'd go to the checkpoint," Jena interjected.

Brock nodded. "Yeah, he not only knows our location, he knows our strengths and our weaknesses."

"The only way to have the advantage is to go after them now. We've got to attack the checkpoint," Galin said. "Then we'll hide in the mountains while we figure out what to do about the keep." Galin jumped down from the table. "Get a squad together to do a recon on the checkpoint. We need to do this right, because those orcs are more experienced and stronger than our fighters."

"You got it."

Galin watched Brock rush out of the medical tent. *I hope I know what I'm doing.*

CHAPTER 15

Tasar Escapes

"Damn it!" Tasar screamed as he stepped in cow dung in the pasture north of Nia. His blue face became redder with each step towards the Wailing Mountains checkpoint. The field was crowded with brown and black cows munching on the long grass. If he had just another second, or had just kept his fat mouth shut, he'd have Galin's head in the sack over his shoulder. But no, he had to show his prey how superior he was to him. Tasar sniffed. At least his mount and equipment were safe at the checkpoint.

Tasar strained his eyes to see the northern road leading out of Nia in the distance. Those 300,000 crowns were the last of the money he needed to get back home to Setan. *At least you don't smell the humans there! Nasty smelly things.* Beldroth took him in when he was a just a young Dark Elf, nearly 110 years ago. Studying under her was an honor—no, a privilege. They even swam in each other's lust and fantasies for over forty years. Chalia was a product of their eternal love, changing their lives forever. Tasar frowned. *Then, that bastard Tanyl came to power with a great plan to over-throw the humans, the Vulwin Elves, and the rest of our ancestral enemies.* That's when he took her from him.

His stomach turned as he remembered their last night together, before she became the slave to Kade, the fraternal twin brother to the king. Even though Kade demanded and wanted to lay with her, Beldroth's heart never left Tasar. She refused Kade at every turn until that orc's ass, Tanyl, forced her to give herself to him.

Tasar stepped over a small rock wall and onto the hard-packed dirt road towards the checkpoint. That night at Staerdale Castle, so long ago, he was among the multitude of mages waging war on the castle under Beldroth's command. He was a proud member of the Darkstriders then; that was before Beldroth was killed by that wench Thea the Loyal, leaving him to raise their daughter alone. Tasar spit on the ground. Soon he'd be able to bring Chalia home, away from this nightmare.

As he cleared the rise, the checkpoint came into view. Its stone walls that extended at least two hundred yards beyond the gatehouse were curved towards the Wailing Mountains. Where the stone walls ended, a wooden fence was erected and it stretched another one hundred yards to the base of the mountains. Tasar smiled. *Finally*.

~

HE WALKED TOWARDS THE GATEHOUSE. Several heavily muscled Feral Orcs blocked his way. They wore chain mail armor underneath their breastplates, with twin axes hanging by their sides. Tasar smiled. "Let me pass."

The largest of the orcs gave Tasar a shove. "No, you must pay me toll first."

Tasar looked at the others nodding in agreement. "There's no toll here."

"You not part of Darkstriders," the orc said. "You pay toll." He reached for his axes. "Your coin or your head."

Tasar rolled his eyes. "I need to see your captain. Now, out of my way." He tried to push his way past them, but was slammed to the ground. Blood dripped from the corner of Tasar's mouth. "What will they do to you when I tell them that you let Galin V get away when he was a mere six miles from here?" Tasar grinned. "How many pieces will Tanyl cut you into? Or will he send you to the seers and watch your blood boil while it's still running through your veins? Oh, how I'll enjoy watching that." He motioned to the others. "I'm sure our great leader will accommodate all of you."

The orcs moved out of his way.

Tasar sniffed as he rushed through the gate. "That's

what I thought." He followed the eastward road for about one hundred yards. Still behind the stone wall and just off to the north side of the road stood a one-story wooden building with a thatched roof. There were two hitching posts outside on either side of the door. He pushed his way into the small building.

Tasar's nose wrinkled as he entered the small wooden building. The rancid odor of Feral Orcs being in a heated enclosed space hit him like a hammer. The once beautiful hardwood floor was pitted, with pools of dried up blood. In the far corner was a pile of broken chairs, right next to a cross, where they would question the humans. The cleanest part of the one-room structure was to his left. It almost seemed out of place. The large oak wooden desk had no scratches, and everything on it was neat and organized. The orc that sat behind it wore his Darkstrider Armor proudly. It was not dented, rather it was unblemished. Tasar smiled. "Good morning."

The enormous greenish-skinned bald Feral Orc looked up. "What do you want?"

Tasar picked up an unbroken chair and placed it in front of the desk. "Do you have a moment?"

"No."

"Good." Tasar slid into the chair, beaming at him. "Captain Xugar, I left my things with you, and your troops did not want to let me pass unless I paid some silly toll."

Xugar looked up. "Who?"

Tasar shrugged. "I didn't ask their names."

"Don't bother me then. Get out."

"I can't," Tasar began. "I need your help and you need mine."

"Too busy," he said without even looking up.

Tasar rubbed his chin. "What would you say if I told you that the young man the Darkstriders have been looking for over the past fifteen years or so is a mere six miles away?"

Xugar looked up. "Where?"

Tasar smiled. "Before I say, we need to come to some agreement. If not, well, my memory isn't what it used to be. It must be my age."

"What do you want?"

"His head, nothing more. I promised it to a client of mine. You may know him, Artis the Black."

Xugar laughed. "That coward? He sold out his own race for a tiny plot of useless land on the other side of the Wailing Mountains. He's a devious piece of work."

"I know, but I did make him a promise."

Xugar sat back. "If you take his head, how do I prove I got him? They won't take my word for it. Would your employer take yours?"

"Good point. Well, you could use the rest of his body, plus all the bodies of his *troops*."

"Troops? What troops?" Xugar demanded.

"Oh, didn't I tell you? He has a training camp south of here and he's got over 500 volunteers. They've been there for a few weeks now," Tasar said. "How would the great Tanyl reward you if you crushed the rebellion before it even got started?"

The orc's eyes glistened as if imagining what he would do with that much wealth. "We'd have to call for reinforcements from Iron Fist Keep. We simply do not have enough troops here."

"How many do you have?"

"Less than fifty," Xugar replied. "If I send a runner out now, the fastest they would get here is seven to ten days."

Tasar frowned. "They'll be gone by then. You do understand that?"

Xugar glared at him. "What would you have me do?"

"They are barely trained and out in the open. Hell, they're training in a cornfield. Our best chance is to take them by surprise."

"Attack? Are you nuts? They have ten times the amount of troops I've got. No, we have to call for reinforcements."

"I'm a pyromancer and I studied under Beldroth," Tasar said.

"*The* Beldroth?"

Tasar nodded. "Yes, *the* Beldroth. My power is just as powerful as hers."

Xugar laughed. "I doubt Beldroth's powers were as powerful as the stories tell us they were. No, we're calling for reinforcements."

"Look, none of them have seen battle before. Can you imagine an entire force facing the mighty Feral Orcs for the first time with fire raining down from the sky? They'd flee like dogs."

"The cost would be too high. How many good orcs are you willing to sacrifice for your ambitions?"

Tasar smiled. "All of them. Aren't you?"

Xugar glared at him. "No, I'm not. I will not waste my men like that."

"What kind of a Darkstrider are you?"

"I'm not. I'm a Feral Orc first, Darkstrider second. I'm loyal to my people and I will serve them the best way I know how. If you have a more realistic idea, then I'll listen. Otherwise, I'm sending for reinforcements. If they're forming an army, we've got to alert Tanyl and the king."

Tasar leaned back in his chair. "Hmm. What if we attack some of them in a way to scare them into thinking all is lost?"

Xugar shook his head. "Warriors would not be fooled by that."

"They're not warriors. They're farmers and merchants."

"And how would we attack only some of them?"

"Well, they know that we know where they are and what they are doing."

"How?"

Tasar blushed. "I failed to kill Galin, that's how. But, it may work to our advantage."

"I see." Xugar took a pipe from his desk drawer and packed it full of tobacco. "What do you think their end goal is? Is Tanyl right?"

Tasar nodded. "Yes, he wants to reclaim the throne and kick us all back to Setan." He leaned closer. "What would you do?"

Xugar lit his pipe and toked it. His eyes almost seemed gleeful as the smoke escaped from his mouth. "Assuming his goal is to dethrone Kade, and that I knew that my location was known to my enemy, I'd move now. Granted, I wouldn't be ready to assault the castle, but perhaps a smaller target. One that could give me a strategic advantage over my enemy. At the same time, I'd take into account the poor training my forces had versus my opponents."

"Where would you go?"

"Well, you'd need to take a place that was secure and where you could raise more forces." He blinked. "I'd go somewhere where my enemy has little interest and is lightly defended."

Tasar raised an eyebrow. "What?"

"Iron Fist Keep. There are few forces there, and this is the only way through the Wailing Mountains. The keep's real purpose is to keep others out of Axain. Tanyl doesn't have enough forces to hold territory beyond the keep. That's why he recruited humans to be Darkstrider knights, to cover those outlying territories that he really doesn't care about."

"What would happen if Iron Fist Keep was properly defended by them?"

"It would take a long siege or an army of mages to breach the walls. Even then, they could hold out a long time and have an escape route so they'd live and fight again," Xugar said. "The cost to us would be enormous."

"They have to come through here, right?" Tasar asked.

Xugar nodded. "What do we do?"

"They'd need to know exactly what's up here, wouldn't they?"

"Sure, I'd send a reconnaissance patrol. Why wouldn't they?"

Tasar's lips twisted into a wicked a smile. "This is what we're going to do."

CHAPTER 16

Ambush

The next morning, Galin was sitting on the ground in his tent with a map spread out in front of him. He had been staring at it for hours as if the passing of time would change his situation. How could he ask barely trained volunteers to recon the checkpoint without going himself? Would that make him a hypocrite? Brock, of course, would say no. Galin's gut didn't believe it. No, not one bit. He sighed.

"Sorry we're late," Jena said as she entered the tent, with Brock and Ellis close behind.

Galin smiled as they sat around the map. "I'm not so sure about this. I feel...like I'm sending them to get killed."

Ellis rolled his eyes. "Please, they're just going to

take a look. Nothing will happen. You worry like an old fishmonger."

"He's right," Brock said. "This should be an easier mission for them."

"Are you saying there is no danger? Really?" Galin asked.

Brock shook his head. "I didn't say that. Of course it's dangerous and yes, you could be sending them to their deaths." His eyes softened. "This is the ugly part of our mission. We can't control everything. Sometimes, we need to have faith in others to do their job."

Jena held Galin's hand. "He's right and you know it."

"Doesn't mean I have to like it," Galin replied. Should he go anyway? His dragon magic would help, at least a little. But, if he went and got captured, it would be over. All those people who believed in him and sacrificed their lives would have died for nothing. No, he could never allow that. He needed a victory to bring the experienced warriors out of the shadows. And it was only a matter of time before the Darkstriders attacked them. No, he had no choice. "When are they coming?"

"I only asked for the squad leader to come," Brock said.

"Who's that?"

Brock scratched his right cheek. "She's from Vebaco. A smart girl and good with a bow. She earned the respect from her squad. I think she'll do great."

Ellis blinked. "A girl?"

Brock glared at him. "A girl saved the kingdom! She

was the best knight I ever knew. I wish I was half as brave as Thea the Loyal."

"Am I in the right—oh, I am," a young woman with long, red hair said. She wore a tan tunic and brown trousers. If it wasn't for her well-defined chest, she could have easily been mistaken for a boy.

Brock motioned her to sit next to him. "Galin, this is Mae Rizik."

"Nice to meet you," Galin said.

Mae's face was solemn. "What am I doing?"

Galin looked into her eyes, as if trying to see into her soul. "Have you killed anyone before?"

Mae shook her head. "No."

"Galin, enough," Brock said.

"But," Mae began, "I can do it. I know I can."

"What about your squad?" Galin asked.

Mae swallowed. "Yeah, they're up for anything." She looked at Brock. "Is there a problem?"

"No, no problem," Galin said. There was no backing out now, he had to send them. Galin pointed on the map. "Here we are, west of Nia."

Mae nodded.

Galin's finger followed the road leaving Nia. "This road goes due north and intersects the only road that crosses the Wailing Mountains. At this intersection, there's a checkpoint. It's guarded by Feral Orcs."

"There could be human Darkstrider knights or Dark Elves, also," Brock said.

"Okay," Mae said.

Galin leaned forward. "We need to know how many there are and what kind."

Mae blinked. "What kind? What do you mean?"

"Knights, war mages, pyromancers, that kind of stuff," Brock said.

"I can do that."

Brock smiled. "I know you can. That's why I picked you."

"Look," Galin said. "All I want you to do is look and come back. Your scouting does us no good if you don't make it back. Understand?"

She nodded.

"There is one more thing. Pretend to be travelers, but stay off the road," Brock said.

"Why?" Mae asked.

Galin sighed. "Dark Elves can take human form and we had one in camp. He nearly killed me. That's why we have to move now."

"How does that affect my mission?"

"They will most likely be on some kind of alert. He may even recognize you." Galin shifted in his seat. "If you keep at a distance, it is less likely you will be stopped or even questioned. Do you understand?"

Mae nodded. "I do."

Brock stood up. "I'll help you get ready." Mae followed Brock out of the tent.

Galin's soft eyes looked at Jena. "I hope I did the right thing."

Jena tried to smile. "You did."

I hope they come back, Galin thought.

~

MAE WORE a green cloak over her chain mail armor with her short sword hanging from her waist and her bow draped across her back. A large man from Nia strolled next to her. His bald head glistened in the afternoon sun. "Sean, how much further?" Mae asked.

"About another mile," Sean Bennett replied. He pointed at the three men and two women following them. "Are we purposefully going for the traveler look? Or are we just poorly disciplined?"

Mae blinked. Was that a serious question or was he still upset about Brock choosing her over him? Sure, when the squad was formed, Sean immediately took charge. His father was a knight or something during Galin IV's rule, before the Darkstriders and Kade the Usurper evicted him from power. How should she respond to that? The truth was that they were that undisciplined because they really hadn't trained. What good would it do to admit it? "No, we're going for the traveler look."

"I see. If we're travelers, why are we walking across this pasture and not on the road? Travelers don't walk over here." Sean pointed at the northern road leading out of Nia. "Real travelers walk on that."

Really? His sarcasm hit Mae like a catapult, there was no escaping it. "Brock said to stay off the roads."

Sean looked back at the others. "What do you all think? Do you want to keep walking on this uneven pasture or do you want to walk on the road?"

"The road," one woman said.

"Wherever the squad wants," a man said.

"My feet hurt," the other woman said. "Let's go on the road."

Without waiting for an order from Mae or even asking her, Sean led the group towards the road. "Come on. She can walk on the pasture if she wants."

"Stop! Brock said to stay off the roads," Mae said. "So, we are staying off the roads."

"Why?" Sean demanded. "What's so dangerous about the road I walked on all my life, even after the Darkstriders took over?"

"There was a Dark Elf in the camp, training with us. They know that we have to make our move now, before we're overrun. If we're on the road and that Dark Elf sees us, he could recognize us."

Sean snorted. "Whatever. We're still walking on the road. Besides, what can one Dark Elf do against all of us?"

Mae looked back at her squad. Surely, they could take out one Dark Elf if they had to, right? It was disobeying orders. There were over five hundred volunteers training at the camp; what were the chances of that Dark Elf recognizing them? Slim, right? Maybe even none? Her aching feet were agreeing with Sean, but her gut said to stand firm. She looked over at the road. It was empty, nothing as far as the eye could see. Besides, if they saw someone coming, they'd have time to turn and run. Mae smiled as her feet won the battle. "Okay, but keep an eye out."

Sean smiled. "I knew you'd see it my way."

Twenty minutes later, Mae was leading her squad up

the road, walking en masse. It was almost like going for a walk with your friends after a long night at the tavern. Eyes were not up ahead nor looking along the sides of the road. No, they were flirting and laughing. All but Mae. She picked up the pace, determined to regain control. "Come on. We're wasting time. We've got a job to do."

"What job?" Sean demanded. "I volunteered and I can leave whenever I damn well please."

Mae stopped and stared right at him. "Sean, don't do this."

"Do what?"

"Stop undermining me! I wouldn't do it to you."

"Hey, lighten up, Mae," a woman said.

"No," Mae snapped. "I won't lighten up. Everyone is depending on us. We're going to be attacking this checkpoint in a few days. It's crucial that we get the information that Galin and Brock need."

Sean blinked. "What do you mean, *attack?*"

"Are you deaf *and* stupid? What do you think it means?"

Sean threw his hands up. "Whoa, I made a promise after too much ale in the Cowardly Owl and, besides, it sounded like fun. But, attacking the Darkstriders? For real?"

Mae nodded.

"You know, being away from camp and so close to home, I'm having second thoughts." Sean smiled at the rest of the squad. "How about you? Sure, it was fun, but now it's just getting too…dangerous."

"Sean! Stop being a coward!" Mae yelled.

Sean knocked Mae to the ground. "I'm not a

coward, just smart, unlike you. I'm going to walk to the checkpoint, get you the information, and then I'm out. Who's with me?"

Mae's heart sank as her entire squad, one by one, joined Sean on the far side of the road. "You're making a huge mistake."

Sean shook his head. "No, were not." He motioned her off the road. "You can watch from a distance if you want, but you're not welcome to come with us."

"But, Sean—" a woman interrupted.

"No, and that's final. Do you want to go back with her?" Sean smiled as she looked away. "That's what I thought. Now, come on."

Mae slipped over the stone wall and into the pasture. She watched the gaggle move north along the road like a herd of sheep. The long grass hid her movements along the wall, keeping them in sight.

Something pulled her eyes to the sky. It looked like embers from a fire, but they were in the sky, high above them. One fell, exploding as soon as it hit the ground, engulfing two of her former squad in flames. Their burning bodies ran off the side of the road, screaming.

Sean drew his sword, as did the remaining three volunteers.

Tears came to her eyes as the sky rained fire, engulfing those who she thought were her friends only a few minutes ago.

Sean dropped to his knees as the two women, wrapped in flames like a blanket, collapsed on the ground, crying out for anyone to help them.

A Dark Elf and fifteen Feral Orcs stood up from behind the stone wall on the far side of the road, just ahead of Sean and the lone survivor. He pointed at the two men and the orcs rushed them.

Sean cried as he surrendered without a fight.

The other man swung his sword, slashing an orc's skin on his arm.

The orc raised its ax and brought it down like a guillotine.

Mae looked away as his headless body fell to the ground. She had to tell Brock about the Darkstriders and…her failure. Mae stayed low and bolted towards the camp.

"Bring that coward back to the checkpoint," Xugar said. "He'll be able to tell us what they're up to."

Tasar nodded. "I concur."

Something caught Xugar's eye, deep in the pasture. "Look, there's another one!" He motioned for his lieutenant.

Tasar pulled his arm down. "No, let her go."

"Why?" Xugar demanded.

His malicious smile grew on his face. "You saw how weak these were. What do you think will happen when she tells everyone what happened here?" Tasar's gaze followed Sean being dragged off by the orcs. "May I assist in the interrogations?"

Xugar grinned. "Of course."

Darkstrider Checkpoint

Galin was pacing around the table in his tent. Jena followed him with her eyes from her seat on the ground. "Pacing won't help. You're going to wear out the ground around the table." She patted the ground next to her. "Come and join me."

Galin smiled. "Sure." As he sat down, Galin gazed into her hypnotic eyes. His soul was hers and hers alone. "Think we'll make it to Iron Fist Keep?"

She snuggled against him as he pulled her closer to his heart. "Yeah, I think so. After all, you've got a promise to keep," Jena grinned. "Or else."

"I just never sent someone out on a…mission before. I don't feel right about it. I should be there with them."

"You know what you just said was a bunch of crap.

When you command and rule, you can't do everything." Her eyes softened. "Now, only now do I really understand how you felt when you lost your mother. All I felt was hatred, anger, and all I wanted to do was kill every last one of them. Nothing else mattered to me but ripping those jerks limb from limb."

Galin blinked. "Jena, I'm sorry. I—"

She put up her hand, silencing him. "No, let me finish."

"Sorry."

Jena's eyes welled up. "Then I nearly lost you. All that hatred made me forget the one and only thing that matters to me in this life and the next; you." Tears started rolling down her cheeks. "When they brought you into my tent, skewered like a hog, my heart nearly died. I can't live without you. You're all I have left."

Galin felt as one with Jena as he wiped away her tears. "I don't want you to travel down that dark road like I did when I killed Shania, my love. I thought my anger would just go away after she was dead. I was wrong. It only got worse. In school, whenever you got hurt or poisoned or whatever, I became enraged, nearly killing myself. That's why Nyna said to not get married until we've won. He felt that if you got hurt, I'd destroy myself with rage." He kissed her forehead. "But, he was wrong. If that really did happen, if I truly lost you, I would already be dead. Your heartbeat is my heartbeat. Your breath is mine. We are one in love, spirit, and body. I cannot live without you, nor do I want to."

Jena beamed at him.

"I love you, I love you more than life itself."

She pushed herself on top of him, kissing him passionately.

"Galin!" Brock yelled as he rushed into the tent. As soon as he saw Jena thrusting her tongue into Galin's mouth, Brock cleared his throat. "There's no time for that. Come quickly, they're back."

Galin shot up. "What's wrong?"

Brock swallowed. "You've got to come out here and see."

He looked over at Jena. "Let's go." They followed Brock outside.

In the clearing, all the volunteers were staring at Mae's ghost-white face. Galin knelt by her side. "Are you all right? Do I need to get Jena?"

Mae shook her head. "I failed. I—"

Galin put his hand over her mouth. "Can we get a little privacy please?"

One by one, all the volunteers returned to their encampments in the wood line.

Galin smiled. "Go ahead."

"They left me. Sean convinced the others ignore me and"—she looked up at Brock—"do what you told us not to do." Mae's face collapsed into her hands.

Jena put her arm around Mae. "It's okay."

"Where are the others?" Galin asked.

Mae looked up with tears flowing down her face. "Dead! All right, you happy now? They're all dead!"

"Are you sure?" Brock asked.

"They took Sean, and the rest were burnt alive or killed by the Feral Orcs."

Galin put his hand on her shoulder. "This is very important, Mae. Please try to concentrate."

She nodded.

"Did Sean know what we were planning to do? Did he know we're going to attack the checkpoint?"

Mae nodded again.

"Damn," Brock said. "They'll know within hours, if they don't know already. We've got no choice. We've got to retreat."

"To where?" Galin demanded. "No, that's not an option. We can't give in that easy."

"What choice do we have?"

Galin's face reddened as he closed in on Brock. "I'm in charge, not you! That's something you need to remember."

Jena leaped to her feet and jumped in between Galin and Brock. "Enough of this crap. You're both men, act like it before I whip the both of you!"

Galin opened his mouth to protest, but nothing came out. He smiled. "She's right."

Jena grinned. "I'm always right."

"What do we do then?" Brock asked.

Both Jena and Mae looked at Galin.

He swallowed. *Well, Galin, what should you do?* "We attack, and we attack right now."

"What? No, I told you what happened," Mae said as she pointed to the volunteers in their encampments. "Think they don't know? They do. I told them. I'm so terrified."

Galin knelt down. "I'll be with you." He stood up

and looked at Jena. "Could you ask them to come over here?"

Jena nodded and hurried off.

"What's your plan?" Brock asked.

"Our people need a victory for confidence in themselves. When Ellis and I went through the checkpoint, there couldn't have been more than twenty or thirty orcs there."

"There's probably more than that. You have to figure the commander and those who weren't on duty," Brock said.

Galin shrugged. "We attack with half the camp and the other half follows up the rear with all our equipment. What do you think?"

Brock grinned. "You're going to be a great king."

Slowly, the volunteers formed a semicircle around Galin. He climbed on top of a cart so everyone could see him. His stomach twisted. He could—he would lead them, and they would win. Galin cleared his throat. "I know you all heard about the patrol. Some of you might think that we don't stand a chance. Others may even think it's better to bow out now, while you're still alive." Galin nodded. "You could do that and I won't stop you. Someday when you're old and have your grandchild on your knee and he asks you what did you do during the great revolution, what will you say? You could say, I ran away at the first sign of trouble. I ran away before I ever saw battle. Or, you could say that you personally gave freedom to the kingdom of Axain from the tyranny by the Darkstriders. The choice is yours."

"We won't all come back!" a man yelled from the crowd.

Galin nodded again. "Yes, that's true. When we win, if you don't make it back, the ballads will sing about your victories or your cowardliness. Which do you want?"

Brock smiled at Galin.

"We're going to attack that checkpoint now, while we still have the upper hand. Half the camp will come with me to attack the checkpoint and the rest will be with Brock to bring up our equipment. Get your stuff together and let's claim our first victory!"

The volunteers cheered. "Galin! Galin! Galin!"

Galin took it all in. Their cheers and blind obedience were like a…drug. No wonder his uncle wanted to be king so badly. He jumped down.

Ellis shook his head. "I always knew you were a cheese ball. Did you really believe all that crap you said?" After a moment, he frowned. "I didn't think so."

Jena held Galin's hand. "You're going to need me."

"I'd have it no other way." Galin looked up at Ellis. "Coming?"

Ellis smacked him on the back. "Think I'd let you take all the loot? Fat chance. Let me get my stuff."

"Is he ever serious?" Jena asked as they watched Ellis walk towards Runt.

Galin grinned. "He's always serious." He took one more look at the poorly trained army on his way towards his tent. Was he doing the right thing?

~

AN HOUR LATER, with Jena and Ellis right next to him, Galin was on Thea, looking back at his "infantry." Well, at least they'd trained for a couple of weeks. They were scared, but pumped. Everyone had lost a relative or friend, or knew someone who had, to those monsters. *Yeah, that would end well, right?* Galin bit his lip. Two hundred fifty volunteers against less than fifty Dark-striders and one pyromancer, Tasar. Just by the pure numbers, they should win, right? Maybe, he should—

Ellis snapped his fingers in front of Galin's face. "Hey, you awake?" He smiled. "You need to stop doing that or people will start to think you're nuts."

Galin grinned. "I *am* nuts."

"That's why I love you," Jena said. She caressed her short swords. "Do I focus on these or healing?"

Galin frowned. Which indeed? She was far more experienced than their volunteers, but she would be very busy just being a healer. Well, maybe. She did say that she could only heal a few times per day, and the rest would be done through conventional methods using bandages. He frowned. Which indeed? "Is there someone who can triage the wounded?"

Jena nodded.

"Stick with us," Galin said as he watched Brock ride up beside him.

"You ready?" Brock asked.

"We are. You?"

"Yeah, we are all set." Brock's eyes softened. "What are you going to do if you get into trouble? How will you signal us?"

"I'll send a rider back if things look like they're going poorly," Galin said.

Brock sighed. "All right. We'll be ready."

Galin watched his adoptive father ride back to his formation of volunteers and carts carrying their camp. "He's worrying."

"Aren't you?" Ellis said. "You're some kind of nut if you're not." He shifted in his saddle. "Better get going before I change my mind."

Galin smiled. "All right." He motioned his "troops" to follow him.

Ellis sighed. "Here we go."

Galin urged Thea north, towards the checkpoint. His face hardened, trying to appear resolute to hide his doubts. Everyone was depending on him and he wasn't going to let them down. Galin led his forces through the northern pasture while replaying how the battle would go in his mind over and over again. He would call up his dragon magic. Yeah, he had to take out the pyromancer, *then* his people would have a chance. But, how would they mitigate the damage Tasar could do until then? Galin looked over his shoulder. His two hundred fifty volunteers were all walking in a single mass, like a mob ready to burn down the magistrate's house. No, that would not do. What if those fire bolts that Mae told him about happened right now? He'd lose half of them, if not more. No, they had to spread out. "Ellis."

"What?" Ellis asked.

"I want you to have our volunteers spread out and put them into three platoons."

"What for?"

"The first wave will come with me and Jena. Once we are engaged, send the second wave, followed by the third. That's the only way we can minimize the damage that Tasar can do to us," Galin said.

Ellis nodded. "Okay, I got it. When do I come in?"

Galin smiled. "With the last wave. I want you to lead them."

"Figures."

"What?"

Ellis grinned. "You just need me to save your ass again, for umpteenth time." He laughed as he turned Runt around towards the volunteers.

Galin halted the formation. He leaned over to Jena. "Let's ride ahead to take a look while Ellis is getting them organized."

"Won't they see us?" Jena asked.

"Yeah, but they won't be able to identify us at that distance." Galin glanced over to Ellis. "We'll be right back!"

Ellis looked up as he was arranging the fighting formations. "What?"

"Trust me." Galin and Jena rode ahead.

They were closer than Galin thought. Near the final rise before the checkpoint there was a stone wall on the edge of the pasture. He jumped down from Thea and crept behind the wall.

"That it?" Jena asked as she joined him.

Galin nodded. "Yeah, it looks the same as when Ellis and I came through it; well, almost." It was different. Now, there were patrols outside the wall on horseback.

"I see at least five on horseback just a hundred yards from the walls."

"Where do we get in?"

Where? Galin swallowed. If they went through the front, the Feral Orcs could escape and warn Iron Fist Keep. They would, of course, send reinforcements. No, that couldn't be it. He looked just beyond the stone walls, closer to the mountains. There was a wooden fence that could be easily jumped over, if not toppled. Yeah, they wouldn't be funneled, either. But, again, the orcs would simply run to Fison, just east of the bridge over the River of Souls, and get reinforcements.

"What do you think? The front or the back?" Jena said. "I think the back would be easier."

Galin shook his head. "No, we're hitting both. Come on." He jumped on Thea and headed back to Ellis and the volunteers.

Thirty minutes later, Galin, Ellis, Jena, and one captain for each of the waves were huddled together. Mae was the captain of the wave with Galin, which made him smile. Maybe this battle would get back her confidence. Galin sketched the checkpoint in the dirt. He pointed to the front. "My and Jena's and Mae's wave will hit them in the front. I should draw out most of their forces and Tasar." He pointed to the opening in the wall that he and Ellis had gone through. "Here is where we will have problems. No matter what happens, we have to push through this point and force the fight to be on the other side."

"Why?" Mae asked.

"That will make them withdraw a little and prevent

Tasar from using some of his magic, like the fire bolts you saw. Once we are engaged with the orcs, he can't use it without hitting the orcs," Galin said.

"What if he doesn't care about them?" Ellis asked.

Galin blinked. He never thought of that. Did it matter? No, Tasar needed the orcs as much as they needed him. So, Tasar was the key. "He needs them too much." He pointed at the wooden fences behind the stone walls. "Ellis, I want you to take the remaining two waves through here and kill every Darkstrider you see. We can't have anyone escape; they'll just bring reinforcements. You push from the mountains towards me and we'll meet in the middle."

"I like it," Ellis said with a grin.

"Right, let's go before we're discovered." Galin mounted Thea and led his forces towards the front of the checkpoint.

After about twenty minutes, they arrived at the stone wall. Galin was on Thea, with a few other mounted volunteers, followed by the masses. About thirty or so volunteers brought their own horses and that gave them an advantage. He should be able to rush the gate, but could he use his dragon magic while on Thea? He'd never done that before. It burned his skin, but what about his horse? Perhaps the thick leather saddle would protect her; maybe. Galin shook it off. "Ready?" he asked Jena.

She held her reins in her left hand and one of her short swords in the other. "Ready."

Galin took one last look. The Darkstriders headed towards the opening in the stone wall. They must have seen them. "Follow me!" Galin urged Thea to charge. She galloped faster than she ever did before. The wind blew so hard it was tough for Galin to keep his eyes open. He forcibly brought back the images of his mutilated adoptive mother in the bedroom and the hatred he had for the Dark Elves. That tingle from his heart began to spread throughout his body. Tiny arcs jumped along his skin and his eyes began to glow. He was barely fifty yards from the entrance and the Feral Orcs were standing in the way with their axes drawn. "Get ready!" He urged Thea to go faster and faster and faster. Galin leaned into Thea, readying for the impact. Behind the Feral Orcs was Tasar. He was kneeling over a small pile of embers, waving his hands and his mouth was uttering an…incantation? Must be.

Galin cracked his reins and targeted Tasar. He wasn't even thinking of the orcs anymore, just that *damned* Dark Elf. Thea tightened up.

The orcs swung at Thea's feet.

She jumped over them, hitting two orcs in the head with her rear hooves as she sailed over them, knocking them down.

Jena's brown horse with the white patch over her left eye was right behind Thea. Tyra bowled over the other two orcs, knocking them to the ground, which were trampled by the other thirty mounted volunteers.

Galin leaped from Thea, taking Tasar to the ground.

"We're through!" Jena slapped Tyra in the butt as she dismounted to face the greenish Feral Orcs. Armed with two short swords, she smiled at her opponent and charged.

Tasar rolled over, trying to push Galin off.

Galin jumped back, bringing his sword down onto Tasar.

Tasar rolled to the left.

Galin frowned as the blade harmlessly bounced off the dirt.

Tasar pulled out a dagger and threw it at him.

Galin screamed as the dagger embedded into his shin. Rage. The hatred flowed through like a raging mountain river. That unforgettable smell of burning flesh reached his nostrils. His blade glowed a bright-red, not the usual white.

Tasar's eyes widened. "Oh, shit!"

Galin slammed his sword into Tasar's right leg, severing it from his body.

Tasar looked down at the wound. It was cauterized. He held his hands up. "Please, please don't."

Galin's darkened face smiled. "No! No mercy for you!"

"Galin! Help!" Jena screamed.

Galin whirled around to see Jena held down by two orcs as a third had its ax raised to slice her in two. He charged at the orc, swinging his glowing blade. The head bounced towards the two holding Jena.

They relaxed their grip as they looked at their friend's head at their feet.

Jena dropped to the ground, grabbing her blades. She arched her back as she thrust the two blades up under their rib cages.

The two orcs fell to the ground.

Jena's face whitened as she saw Galin. "Get control of it. You're killing yourself!"

Galin looked down. His forearms were smoldering. He turned back to Tasar. He was gone. The only piece that remained was his severed leg. "Damn it!" His eyes glowed a bright red as he turned towards Xugar and twenty other Feral Orcs.

"What kind of sorcery is this?" Xugar yelled. His great ax rested between his hands. "I'm going to kill you!" He raised his ax.

A battle cry sounded behind him. He looked over his shoulder and saw Mae lead her wave into the checkpoint. They rushed by them, engaging the Feral Orcs all around them. Galin smiled a wicked smile as he glared at Xugar. "I don't think so."

"Galin!" Jena yelled.

Galin charged.

Xugar swung his ax, nicking Galin's right calf.

Galin fell to the ground.

"No!" Mae yelled as she bolted towards Xugar.

The orc swung his great ax.

Mae looked down as the ax slit her belly wide open and she fell to the ground.

"Mae!" Galin yelled as he rolled to his knees.

Xugar looked down.

In a single, fluid motion, Galin swung his sword, severing both legs, and ran Xugar through.

The huge orc dropped its ax.

Galin looked at his skin. He had to get rid of the energy. He focused all his rage and hatred and anger on the Feral Orc. He placed his hands on its corpse. Galin screamed. Instantly, the greenish skin dried up and his body cracked in a million fragments. All the dragon magic energy was gone. He looked over at Mae, but Jena was already healing her. He leaped to his feet to fight the next orc. But, there were none left. Ellis had already brought his two waves around the back. They had won.

"We get them all?" Ellis asked as he jumped off of Runt.

Galin shook his head. "No, Tasar got away." He looked down at the severed leg by his feet. "Well, most of him."

Ellis grinned. "I guess he won't forget you." He touched Galin's burnt skin. "You've got to do better if you're going to make it out of this."

Jena grabbed Galin's arm. "Are we done?"

"Yeah, I think so." Pain shot through Galin's leg as he pulled out the dagger. "We won't have much time."

"Lay down," Jena ordered.

"What?"

"I need you to lay down, so I can heal you."

"I don't—"

"You're wounded!" Jena smacked him. "Lay down or I'll smack that burnt skin of yours."

Galin blinked. She wasn't kidding, that was for sure. "Okay." He laid down and his eyes veered back towards the Wailing Mountains. *We might actually win.*

CHAPTER 18

Drusas

Hours later, Galin, Brock, Ellis, and Jena led their volunteers up the steep mountain road. Just over the last rise, where they could see Iron Fist Keep, Galin brought them due north. Somewhere between one and two miles off the road, they found an ideal location to set up their camp.

Galin stood outside of his tent. They'd found one of the few, if not the only, flat areas of any decent size. Tall pine trees surrounded the clearing like sentries warning off curious eyes. There was a stream big enough for all their needs running along the northern edge. The likelihood of finding such a place, so close to Iron Fist Keep, was incalculable. It was almost prophetic.

Jena's medical tent, Brock's and Ellis's tents, were

all right next to Galin's, with a small fire between them all. Ellis was pulling out his pots for dinner. "Are you going to just stand there?" Ellis asked.

"What?" Galin asked.

Ellis motioned towards Jena's and Brock's tents. "Go and get them for dinner. It doesn't take me long to fry up some rabbit."

"I—"

Ellis rolled his eyes. "Damn, Galin, I swear you'd starve without me."

Galin smiled. "You're probably right." Galin stuck his head in both of their tents and called them to come out by the fire. He sat down next to Ellis, who already had a pan with a sliced-up rabbit over the fire. "They're coming."

"About time you did *something* useful," Ellis said with a grin.

"Did I miss something?" Jena asked as she took a seat right next to Galin.

Galin shook his head. "No, Ellis is being Ellis again."

"Smells good. I'm glad we brought him along," Brock said with a smile.

Ellis flung a piece of fat at Brock as he sat down, hitting him in the face. "I'm not your personal chef." As the fat ran down Brock's cheek, Ellis couldn't hold his frown for long before he started to laugh.

Galin and Jena laughed, too.

Brock glared at him. "Not funny." He wiped the slimy fat off his face.

Galin got control of himself. "Okay, okay, it's not funny."

"We've got some serious things to talk about, Galin. We're not done yet," Brock said. "That carnage we left behind will be discovered by the Darkstriders soon, if they haven't already."

Ellis put some rabbit on a plate and handed it to Brock. "Why are you always so gloomy? We've just won our first battle. You should be proud, not scared. I mean, we *kicked* their butt."

"They're not the only ones who'll see it," Jena said. "Those people who want to fight the Darkstriders will see it, too."

Galin nodded. "Why shouldn't we want both sides to see it? I say we make it worse."

"What do you mean?" Ellis asked as he handed Galin and Jena a plate.

Brock raised an eyebrow.

Jena looked right at Galin.

Galin swallowed. How indeed? Again, he'd opened his big mouth before really thinking it through. It was too late now. "We hit them along the road to Iron Fist Keep. I hope the Darkstriders do send more Feral Orcs. We can ambush them on that narrow mountain road at a place of our own choosing."

Brock nodded. "That would isolate them." He laughed. "Hell, Tanyl and Kade might think that there is a huge army out here, far more than we've actually got."

"How does that help us with Iron Fist Keep?" Ellis asked. "Surely, they'd hear about ambushes so close to them. Mages can teleport you know, like Tasar."

"We don't know that's what happened," Jena said.

"Yes we do," Galin said. "There's no other explanation for what happened. But, I say that it doesn't matter. If they send out patrols, let them march right past us and return, only to report that there is no army in the mountains."

"They could just button up the keep," Ellis said.

Brock shook his head. "No, if they did without a real good and visible reason, they would lose control of Drusas, Qrento, not to mention Ithsein. They have to keep the trade flowing towards Port Eldham. If they don't, what's the use of occupying Axain?"

Galin nodded. "There isn't one." He took a bite of his rabbit.

"How do we take the keep?" Jena asked. "We can't just go riding in like we did the checkpoint."

Galin looked at Brock. "How did they take Staerdale Castle?"

"Magic tore the walls down, and treachery. There were lots of Dark Elves already within the walls, even before the attack," Brock replied. "We were all betrayed. They must have been planning it for decades."

Galin sniffed. "We don't have that much time."

"Why not take a look around? Or find someone who's been there," Ellis said.

Brock sipped some water from his wineskin. "I think we don't have enough if they really want to fight. Remember, this is a strategic piece of terrain. I'm sure complacency reduced their numbers, but the keep is built right into the mountain and the road goes right through the gate. Any force of any reasonable size must pass through it. Sure, a few could slip past them, but not enough to take the keep."

Galin blinked. "What if their army wasn't there?"

"What the hell are you talking about?" Brock asked. "Why wouldn't they be there?'

Galin glared at him.

"Well, with minimal soldiers at the keep, after we get through the walls, we should have no problems."

"Me, Jena, and Ellis will slip past Iron Fist Keep and go to Drusas," Galin began. "We'll find someone who's been inside the keep and find out how many Darkstriders are there. We'll also find some volunteers to stir some trouble up in Drusas to draw some of their forces out. Once we take the keep, we move into Drusas and liberate the town."

Ellis smiled. "Liberators. I like that. Do liberators get a lot of loot?"

Galin glared at him.

"Sorry." Ellis looked away.

Brock shook his head. "I don't like it. It won't work."

"What do you think we should do?" Ellis asked Galin.

"Find someone who's been inside and knows how to open the gate," Galin said. "That should give us an advantage."

Brock frowned.

"What about two armies?" Jena asked. "Attacking both sides at once?"

"No, no time to train other volunteers. Besides, we have no place to train them," Brock said.

Galin frowned. "He's right. We'll find some people who can help us bring the gates down." He grinned. "Besides, if it is the prophecy, we can't lose." He held Jena's hand and smiled.

"Besides conducting ambushes, what do you want us to do when you're gone?" Brock asked.

"I want you and Mae to train our soldiers—"

"Volunteers," Brock corrected.

Galin shook his head. "No, after what they did at the checkpoint, they are soldiers."

Brock nodded.

"Train them how to take a keep, how to fight as a unit in close quarters, etcetera."

"Okay," Brock said. "I can do that."

Galin looked at Ellis and Jena. "We'll leave in the morning." He took Jena's hand and smiled.

"When will you be back?"

"Soon." Galin and Jena went into Galin's tent.

T HE NEXT MORNING, Galin, Jena, and Ellis rode down a narrow and steep trail down the Wailing Mountains. It reminded Galin of the hunting trail he and Brock used to use when they were setting rabbit traps in Sarun Grove, just north of where Crey Village used to be. The closer they got to the bottom, the thicker the trees became. After several hours, they finally reached the bottom.

Galin and Thea pushed their way through pine

saplings until they reached an enormous field of long fescue grass. "Coming?"

"Ouch!" Ellis yelled. "Do you have smack me with every branch, Jena?"

"Sorry," Jena said as she emerged from the rows of saplings. "I guess we're here."

Ellis tossed a small pine branch to the ground. "Remind me not to ride behind you again."

"Next time, don't ride so close," Jena replied.

Galin rolled his eyes. "Stop it already. Come on, we don't have a lot of time and…we've promised a lot."

"No, *you* promised a lot. Not me," Ellis said.

Galin's eyes followed the tree line south; he pointed at Iron Fist Keep. "Look at it." Its single tower stood like a giant watching over little children at play. It was halfway up the mountain, with walls in front and behind. They stretched for 800 yards and both directions. In the center of the walls, right underneath the tower, were iron portcullises.

"That thing is huge," Ellis said. "No way we can take that."

"It does look impressive."

Jena rolled her eyes. "Please, the size of the tower doesn't matter. Let's go already." She cracked her reins and Tyra galloped towards the town off in the distance.

"I wish I had a tower like that," Ellis said.

Galin laughed. "Stop drooling and come on." They both followed Jena's lead.

About twenty minutes later, they reached the outskirts of Drusas. Rising up from the center of the town was a three-story stone manor. Smaller wooden houses with thatched roofs surrounded it. Galin led Jena and Ellis onto the road into town.

It reminded Galin of Crey Village. People were rushing around, and the smell of fresh-baked bread overcame him. Thea trotted along the hard-packed dirt road towards the town square. The center of town was just outside the manor and there was a public well in the middle of the square. Merchants had booths, and some simply sold their wares off the back of their carts. There were merchants who sold bread, jewelry, weapons, scrolls, magic components, and there was even a fishmonger. The unique odors from the fishmonger's selection of trout and bass hanging from the rack above her booth made Galin pinch his nose. "Yup, just like Crey Village."

"Where do we start?" Ellis asked.

Jena yawned. "I'm tired."

"Let's find an inn. The horses need rest," Galin said.

"The horse? What about me?" Ellis said.

The only two-story building on the square was on the far side. There was a pile of broken furniture off to the right side. A wooden side hung above the door. It read "The Dire Stag Bar." Galin pointed at the bar. "They may have a room."

"Why do you say that?" Jena asked.

Ellis rolled his eyes. "How many two-story bars do you know that don't have rooms?"

Jena frowned.

"Come on," Galin said as he directed Thea towards the Dire Stag.

A woman screamed.

Galin whirled around. Behind them, two Feral Orcs were tearing the clothes off a young woman, right next to the fishmonger. His eyes widened as he saw the people close to her turn their backs, as if not to get involved. "Come on!" He cracked the reins and Thea bolted towards the Feral Orcs.

"Those pricks!" Ellis said as Runt galloped towards the orcs.

"Leave her alone!" Galin drew his sword and leaped from Thea's back onto the orc that was tearing off the woman's clothes, knocking him to the ground.

In a single motion, Ellis whipped out his daggers and flung them at the orcs holding the woman down. Both of them found their mark, embedding themselves into its eye sockets. Ellis leaped down from Runt to retrieve his weapons.

"I'll kill you!" Its greenish skin reddened. The orc reached for the ax hanging from its belt and swung at Galin.

Galin sidestepped, raising his sword. He swung at the orc's head.

The orc ducked and charged at Galin, knocking the sword from Galin's grasp.

Galin stared at the ax raised above his head. He had no sword, nothing to block the blow.

The orc reeled back in pain as it reached for the short sword in its back as it fell over.

"Thought I lost you," Jena said as she helped Galin up.

"Thanks." Galin looked down. The mostly naked woman was sobbing.

Jena knelt down next to her. "Shh, we're here to help." She helped the woman up.

Galin took off his cloak and wrapped it around the woman. "Let's go inside somewhere and get you cleaned up."

"I'm Kathy," the black-haired woman said. Her wet, brown eyes sagged. "Thank you."

Galin led them towards the Dire Stag. Jena grabbed both Tyra's and Thea's reins and passed them to Ellis. "Can you tie off the horses?"

"I suppose," Ellis said.

Galin pushed his way through the crowd inside the Dire Stag. Unlike the taverns in Nia and Vebaco, the Dire Stag was a mess. Floorboards were cracked and the tables had been nailed back together numerous times. There were no stools around most of the tables, as if they had been used for weapons in nightly brawls.

"What a dump!" Ellis said as he followed Galin, Jena, and Kathy.

Galin brought Kathy to the bar. The bartender was a stout man with a curled mustache. "Where can I take her to get cleaned up?"

The bartender's face dropped as he looked into her eyes. "What happened?"

"Orcs, uncle. The orcs tried to take me!" Kathy said. Her face darkened. "And no one helped me!"

"Uncle?" Jena asked.

"I'm William," the bartender said. He motioned to the beer wench at the end of the bar. "Megan, can you take over for a bit?"

The young brown-haired girl smiled. "Yes, Father."

"Bring her into the back," William said.

They followed William through a door behind the bar. They walked through the storage room, which was stacked with wooded cases of wine and kegs of ale. William brought them to his office at the far end of the storeroom. It was small, and the walls were lined with cabinets and shelves and bookcases filled with ledgers. "Sit down, Kathy," William said as he motioned her to the puffy chair behind the wooden desk. He began to rummage through the cabinets. "I think I have some clothes here, somewhere."

"What happened? Why did they attack you?" Jena asked.

Kathy shrugged. "I don't know. I was just walking by and they...they grabbed me." Kathy's face collapsed into her hands as she began to sob.

"What's going on here?" Galin asked. "These Darkstriders seem...different."

William bit his lip. "I am grateful to you for saving my niece. Now please, leave us alone. We don't want any trouble from them or Artis the Black."

"Who?" Ellis asked.

"The governor," William replied as he pulled out a tunic and a pair of pants. "Kathy, I know these are men's clothes, but they'll do until you get home."

Galin blinked. Artis the Black? He'd hired Tasar to kill him. The pieces were beginning to fit into place. What would the reward be for the governor who killed the prophesied boy king and saved the Darkstriders from the prophecy? "Is he human? It sounds like a human knight's name."

William shook his head. "He's barely human. After the Darkstriders took over, a lot of us fought back." His face darkened. "He hunted down and killed most of us who stood up to them. I'd give anything to see his head at the end of a stick. As far as the orcs go, yes, they are different. They don't exactly send their best out here."

"They're undisciplined? Is that what you're saying?"

"Do you really have to ask that? What's wrong with you, boy? You think the attack on Kathy was unique? No, it happens every day and sometimes," his sad eyes looked at Kathy, "sometimes the women don't survive the assault. Those who do, well, some of them wish they were dead."

Galin studied William. Should he tell who him who he was? William obviously had no loyalty to the Darkstriders, nor to Artis the Black. If what he said was true, the whole town might come to his side. "Is there a barracks in town?"

William shook his head. "No, they come down from the keep."

"Good-bye, Uncle," Kathy said as she headed for the door.

"Ask James to go with you. He's upstairs," he replied.

"I will." Kathy closed the door behind her.

"James?" Jena asked.

"My son," William replied.

Galin looked at Jena, as if asking her opinion. After she nodded, he turned back towards William. "I am Galin V of Ravenward, the nephew of Kade the Usurper."

William blinked. "It's not possible. The prince was killed when Staerdale Castle fell."

Galin shook his head. "No, Brock and Sally Feran smuggled me out of the castle before it was lost. Thea the Loyal saved my life. I—"

"Thea the Loyal?" William smiled. "I haven't heard that name in a very long time."

"Did you know her?"

William nodded. "I did. I fought with her at Nightfall Meadows. Well, I was a squire then. My master died at Port Eldham. I got my family and ran until I came to Drusas to start over."

"Did you know my father?"

"Not personally, but I saw him fight. He was courageous and a fair man. His brother was always a hothead, but he became twisted when Beldroth came into his life. We didn't know why until after it was all over." William sat down behind the desk. "Why are you here?"

"I'm raising an army to take back the throne," Galin replied.

William laughed. "Really? Not possible."

"It is. We are going to take Iron Fist Keep to cut off everything east of the Wailing Mountains from them."

"You stroll into town and expect to get folks who've been terrorized by these…these *things* to attack a fortified keep? You're out of your mind."

Galin shook his head. "No, I have five hundred soldiers in the mountains, preparing for the attack right now. I'm here to find someone who's been inside it. Someone who knows the layout and how to raise the portcullis so my soldiers can rush inside."

William studied Galin. "You're serious."

"He's too serious," Ellis said.

"Ellis!" Jena said as she smacked him in the shoulder.

William tugged at his chin. "I can help you, maybe even help you get more fighters. Some of us who raised up against them before are still around. Artis the Black didn't get all of us. Where are you staying?"

"We don't have a room yet," Jena said.

William tossed two keys to Galin. "Here's two rooms. I'll make some inquiries for you, okay?"

Galin nodded. "Sure, I'll see you later then." He looked back at William as he walked through the storeroom. *Did I make a mistake?*

Captured

The next night, Galin, Jena, and Ellis were sitting at a round table near the corner across from the bar. The tavern was packed wall-to-wall with people; no orcs or Dark Elves, just people. Smoke from pipes filled the air, stinging Galin's nose. A trio dancing and playing lutes were on a raised platform in the back of the room.

"Here you go," Megan said as she placed an ale in front of each of them.

"Thank you," Galin said.

"Your dinner will be out soon." She rushed over to the next table.

"I hate waiting," Ellis said.

"We have to give him a chance, Ellis," Jena said. "He knows the people here better than we do."

A thin young woman with light-brown hair and brown eyes came over to their table.

Ellis smiled as he looked up at her. "Hi."

"I want to personally thank you for saving poor Kathy," the woman said.

"It was the least we could do. I'm Ellis."

She shook his hand. "I'm Lena Blunt. May I sit?"

"I don't know," Galin said. "We're expecting some company."

Jena shifted in her seat.

Galin gazed at Ellis' infatuated eyes and smiled. Ellis was looking at Lena just like he looked at Jena, pure love and admiration. Could this be the one for him? Perhaps? Galin cleared his throat. "Lena, do you live in Drusas?"

Lena nodded. "I've lived here all my life. My parents were artisans before"—she tore her eyes away as they welled up with tears—"before *they* took over."

Ellis touched her hand, which she made her smile. "Maybe it won't always be that way."

"Yes it will. There's nothing that can stop it."

"I know—"

Galin glared at Ellis. "Hey, some things are private." His eyes shifted over at Lena. Who was she? Unlike the rest of the townsfolk, she was dressed in much finer clothes than William or the others in the Dire Stag. His eyes looked down at her hands. They were decorated with jewelry embedded with precious stones and an emerald bracelet. She was obviously much better off than the rest of the town. He leaned forward. "Was your family wealthy?"

Ellis blinked. "Where did that come from?"

"It's okay," Lena said. "No, they weren't. I've become successful since the Darkstriders took over. I did what I had to do to survive in today's world. No different than you, Galin V of Ravenward."

"How did you know that?" Jena demanded.

Lena smiled at she rose to her feet. "I didn't, until now." She threw her nose up in the air and hurried out the door.

"I don't like this," Jena said with a quiver in her voice.

"Me either," Ellis said. "But, damn, she was hot."

"Things may have just gotten worse," Galin said. "We're on our own out here. We've got to be careful."

William walked over to the table carrying three plates overflowing with food. "What did Artis the Black's girlfriend want?" he asked as he placed the food in front of them.

Galin looked towards the door. "She knows who I am." He glared at William. "How would she know that?"

"I didn't tell her, but this is a small town. When I asked folks about aiding in your cause, it's not unconceivable that word got around to them." William suddenly looked uneasy. "They know where you are, that much is certain."

"We don't have a lot of time. Maybe a few days, at most," Ellis said. He plopped a spoonful of mashed potatoes into his mouth.

"He's right, Galin," William said. "I'd stay in town no longer than absolutely necessary." His eyes brightened.

"Besides, I found someone that meets your requirements."

Galin leaned forward. "Who?"

William smiled. "The sheriff and his wife. He used to be a knight under your father and his wife is a pyromancer."

"Really?" Ellis asked.

Galin rubbed his chin. "We definitely could use both of them."

"They'll be here in an hour or so. Just to join you for an ale or two," William said as he headed back towards the bar.

A knight and a pyromancer? Could Odella smile on their fortune anymore? Galin remembered Brock telling him about the pyromancers during battle when he was just a boy. They could bring down fire from the sky or shoot fire bolts at an enemy or, if there were enough of them, melt keep walls, just like the Darkstriders did to Staerdale Castle. Even if the sheriff's wife was powerful, one pyromancer couldn't do that. But, she could definitely help. Galin sipped his ale. The larger question that rattled around his mind was, did he have enough soldiers? He never took a keep before and they had no real idea how many Darkstriders were inside, or even how to breach the walls, after they closed those portcullises. Talking like a hero and leader was one thing, actually doing it was completely different. Maybe he should learn to pray.

As the hour passed, the Dire Stag got even more crowded. Anyone with upper class dress was escorted out, and the folks on the lower end of the social ladder were brought inside. It was almost like being successful and wealthy in that time of darkness marked you as a sympathizer or a collaborator. Was it true? Maybe, maybe not.

Galin's eyes bounced from head to head, looking for—what? Something suspicious? If so, it was him. These people were just having a good time, that's all, right? Yeah, that had to be it.

William emerged from the crowd with a six-foot-tall muscular man wearing a chain mail shirt, and a thin woman wearing flowing red robes just behind him. He showed them to the empty chairs across from Galin. "Please, sit down."

Galin looked up.

"Galin V of Ravenward, this is our Sheriff, Karl, and his wife, Abby," William said. "I'll leave you to discuss your business." William disappeared into the crowd.

Karl ran his fingers through his shoulder-length, greasy, brown hair, as if trying to figure out what to say. He leaned into the table, towards Galin. "Are you really who you say you are?"

"Yes."

Abby's blue eyes twinkled as she brushed her blond bangs away from her eyes. "How are you alive? How did you escape the castle?"

Galin shifted in his seat. How, indeed? Why wouldn't everyone who he asked to join his cause ask the same question? Of course, they would. Wouldn't he? "I was saved by Thea the Loyal and Brock and Sally Feran. Brock and Sally raised me as their own in Crey Village, just south of here, along the coast."

Karl motioned the beer wench to bring over some ale. He looked right into Abby's eyes, as if asking her permission or opinion about...something. He swallowed. "There are more people here that can help than you realize."

Galin leaned back in his chair. "Go on."

"There are no Darkstriders here. The ones they do send come from the keep. They rape our women and our men. As soon as they're done, they slit their throats. The Feral Orcs are ruthless and cruel," Karl said. "They send human Darkstrider knights beyond the keep and Drusas."

Jena nodded. "Galin, remember when the Darkstriders first came to Crey Village? They were human."

"And Dark Elves," Ellis added.

"But, no orcs. Those Dark Elves were looking for me," Galin said. He looked into Karl's tired eyes. "We're taking the keep."

"When?"

"Soon. That's why we need someone who knows the inside of it. We can't lay siege to it; the Darkstriders would send reinforcements and overpower us."

"Why Iron Fist Keep?" Abby asked.

Galin smiled. "This keep is the only way to move large formations of troops across the Wailing Mountains. Even then, they cannot mass forces on the other side of the keep. The roads are surrounded by high ground, making them great targets for ambushes and striking them at a distance with long bows. Also, once we have the keep, we can clear out the human Darkstrider knights with ease. Our goal is to have everything east of the Wailing Mountains free of the Darkstriders."

Karl nodded. "I see. How many soldiers do you have?"

"The three of us and five hundred more in the mountains. They are being trained by Brock as we speak."

Karl sent a concerned glance at Abby, who just looked away. He shook his head. "That's not enough. They have around one hundred fifty Feral Orcs inside and only a few venture out of the keep. Every time you attack a keep or a castle, you need siege weapons and ten times the number of troops because the losses are enormous when you're attempting to breach the walls."

"But, it can be done, Karl," Abby said. "What's worse? Staying here and doing nothing or helping the rightful king regain the throne from that traitor?" She tapped her stomach. "What kind of world do you want *our son* to grow up in?"

"Are you having a baby?" Jena asked.

Abby nodded. "We are."

"I want our son to grow up, period. Not to go after some wild dream from long ago." His eyes drooped. "Look, I'm sorry. I'll tell you what I know, but we can't help you."

"Why not?" Abby demanded.

Karl glared at her. "What happens when he fails? They'll come back here and take it out on all of us!"

Ellis yawned. "You're just a coward, admit it."

"Ellis, knock it off!" Jena yelled.

Galin raised his hands, silencing everyone. "You

don't have to come with us. Giving us the information is fine."

"No," Abby said. "Karl, I am going to help them, with or without you."

"You can't! You're carrying our child. I won't let you."

"Stop it!" Galin yelled. "I will not be the cause of you two getting divorced or slitting each other's throats."

"Sorry," Karl and Abby said in unison.

"Okay, what about the others? You mentioned that there were other fighters that may consider helping us," Galin said.

Karl nodded. "That is so, and they are waiting for my assessment on your plan. They may be fighters, but they won't fight unless the plan has a decent chance of succeeding." Karl lowered his voice. "What's your plan?"

Galin smiled. "If we can get fighters on both sides of the keep, we would draw out some of the Feral Orcs to fight between the keep and Drusas while my soldiers attack the keep from the west. A small team will sneak inside the keep and open the western portcullis, enabling my forces to flood the keep."

"That could work," Abby said.

"I agree. All right, after you take the keep, what then?" Karl asked.

Jena and Ellis both stared at Galin.

"Well, we're going use Iron Fist Keep as a base of operations to eliminate the Darkstriders east of the Wailing Mountains, while we recruit and train a larger army to take Staerdale Castle."

Karl grinned. "I see you have it all figured out."

"What do you think? Will you help us?"

Karl and Abby nodded as they rose from the table. "All right, we'll talk to them. I'll give you an answer very soon."

"Thank you," Jena said.

"Bye," Abby said as they vanished in the crowd.

Galin took a swig of ale. "Time for bed?" he asked Jena.

"Yeah." She smiled at Ellis. "Goodnight."

The two of them waded through the crowd until they reached the stairs to their room.

JENA WAS SNUGGLED against Galin with her head on his chest. Their room was barely big enough for the bed and the chair they threw their clothes and weapons on. Galin pulled her in tight, closer to his heart. He loved snuggling more than anything else. He ran his fingers through her hair.

She smiled. "We'll have children one day; one day soon."

"I hope so," Galin said. "We've got to get married first."

"Right after we take the keep, you promised."

He grinned. "I did, didn't I?"

Jena looked right into his eyes, stripping him of his will. "I love you, Galin."

"I love you." He kissed her.

The door flew open. Three Feral Orcs and Lena charged inside.

Galin and Jena shot up, only to be knocked back down by the orcs. Galin glanced at his sword.

"Not nice," Lena said.

"Yeah, human not nice," said an orc as it slammed the hilt of its ax into Galin's temple.

"Jena!" Galin screamed. Spots! At first, there were only a few and then…his world went black.

CHAPTER 20

Torture

Artis the Black sat behind his mahogany desk in his office. There was a half-empty bottle of whiskey next to a small glass in the center, right next to Artis. A smile stretched from ear to ear. He'd got what Tanyl desired most and had failed to find for the past fifteen years. Ever since the fall the Staerdale Castle, that Dark Elf had been looking under every rock and tortured anyone who might know Galin V of Raven-ward's location. How many people died, simply because they didn't know? He sniffed. To think, Tasar was supposed to be the best independent contractor in the kingdom. Ha! His failure merely amplified how Artis the Black was superior to all of them. *Yeah, Tanyl will come crawling on his knees to get Galin.*

Artis smiled. Tanyl would give him anything he

wanted; a title, lands, and more power. The Dark Elves had no interest in anything east of the Wailing Mountains, otherwise they would actually be out here. No, instead they send troublesome Feral Orcs and human Darkstrider knights. He tugged at his chin. How would he bring Galin to him? Alive was out of the question. He was far too dangerous. Lena told him about Galin's magic. If he promised Tanyl Galin alive and he escaped en route, it would be Artis that would be tortured, not the prince.

He sipped his whiskey. Most mages needed to speak, so, if Galin was hanged, could he call up his power? The prophecy said that the boy king would not use spell components or need to speak incantations to bring forth his power. He poured himself another glass of whiskey. *Maybe if we blindfolded—*

Knock. Knock.

"Come in," Artis said as put the whiskey in a desk drawer.

Lena led Tasar into Artis' office.

Tasar glared at Artis. "Governor, you called for me? I'm not some dog that can be summoned by the snap of your fingers."

Artis grinned. "And yet you're here." His eyes glanced down at Tasar's newest addition, a peg leg where his right leg used to be. "Well, I see he outmatched you." He settled back into his plush chair. "So, the rumors were true."

"What rumors?"

"The boy whipped you and the Feral Orcs at the checkpoint on the other side of the Wailing Mountains." He pulled out another glass. "Would you like one?"

Tasar nodded. "Sure."

Artis poured four fingers of whiskey into both glasses. He pushed one over to Tasar. "I didn't summon you. I recalled you."

Tasar sipped his whiskey. "What's the difference?"

"A great deal. I recalled you because I no longer need your services. I have succeeded where you have failed."

"You can't do that! We had an arrangement." Tasar slammed back the rest of the whiskey in his glass. "I won't allow it."

Artis merely smiled at him. "Yes, I can, and I did."

Tasar jumped to his feet. "Fine, I'll be on my way then."

Artis clapped his hands. "No, not yet."

The door opened and three large men grabbed Tasar by the arms, lifting him off the ground.

"What betrayal is this?" Tasar demanded.

"It's a matter of the deposit. Since you never even came close to completing the task, I want it back."

Tasar shook his head. "No, you cannot go back on our arrangement. That deposit was mine whether I got him or not. That was the agreement."

One of the men punched Tasar in the stomach, knocking the air out of his lungs.

Tasar snarled at Artis. "I will kill you. I swear upon your mother's grave."

Artis blinked. "She's not dead."

Tasar grinned. "I know."

Artis waved him off. "Gentlemen, help Tasar find his purse and collect my crowns."

Tasar screamed as they dragged him outside.

"Are you sure that was wise?" Lena asked as she entered the room. "He is quite a capable assassin."

"Used to be, Lena, he used to be." Artis shrugged. "Now, he's got a peg leg and walks with a limp. I should just put him out of his misery."

Lena shook her head. "You can't. If you execute a Dark Elf, Tanyl will have your head."

"And yours," Artis said. "Don't forget that." He threw up his hands. "Enough about that has-been, Tasar. Tell me about our guests."

"We have Galin V of Ravenward and his two companions, Jena and Ellis, in the dungeon. We had to separate them and threaten Galin that we would kill Jena if he used his dragon magic."

Artis raised an eyebrow. "Dragon magic?"

"Yes, the Ellis boy told us. He took some…convincing, but he spilled everything in the end," Lena said.

"Okay, go on."

"It seems Galin wills his power to materialize, but it's purely through emotion. He can control it now."

"Now?"

Lena nodded. "He spent over a year at Tadus School of Magic learning from Nyna."

Artis got up and looked out the window onto the market square. "Did Ellis tell you what the plan for Galin's army is? Or where they are right now?"

"No, he said he doesn't know," Lena said.

"And you believe him?"

"No, but that's what he told me."

Artis took a sip of whiskey. "Is Galin ready for me? I do want to meet him."

Lena nodded.

"Let's go." Artis hurried out of the room, with Lena close behind.

THE LIGHT from the setting sun shined through the barred window in Galin's cell. He was sitting on his lumpy bed with his hands and feet shackled to the bed. He'd heard screams earlier. They sounded like Ellis, but he couldn't be sure. Did he bring his lifelong friends to their death? Was it arrogance that got them captured? Why did this happen? Didn't the prophecy say that he would win? Wasn't that the reason the Darkstriders feared him so much? No, that wasn't it. Galin was the prophesied boy king, he was certain of that. Someday, he would be king. His eyes strained as the last of the sunlight was drawn from the cell.

"Galin V of Ravenward," Artis said as he entered the cell. "This is the first time I've met a member from that royal family in a very long time." He looked back at the two guards standing at the open door. "Wait outside."

"Yes, Governor," they replied as they closed the cell door.

Galin stared through Artis. How much could he believe anything that Artis the Black would say? Galin sniffed. None of it. "Why did you hire Tasar to kill me?"

Artis pulled a stool from the corner and sat across

from Galin. "Well, you're a valuable commodity to Tanyl."

Galin blinked. He'd heard that name before, but where? "Who's that?"

Artis laughed. "You mean you don't know? He happens to be the Dark Elf in charge of the Darkstriders in Axain. It was Tanyl that arranged the killing of your mother and father, not to mention that foolish knight, Thea the Loyal." Artis smirked. "They should call her Thea the Stupid."

"If I'm so valuable to them, why am I still here? Shouldn't I be on my way to Staerdale Castle by now?"

"No, that would be foolish on my part, young man. You may be chained up, but you possess dragon magic. You're far too dangerous to live. I'll deliver your body to them. That should be enough to get what I want."

Galin lunged at Artis, but the chains threw him back onto the bed. "What was your price to sell out your own kind? I heard you got wealthy by betraying everyone around you. You're worse than Feral Orcs and Dark Elves! You don't see them selling out their brothers and sisters for table scraps!"

"I see." Artis leaned forward. "You've got a pretty narrow and one-sided opinion of me. I did what I had to do to survive, just like I am doing again. Sure, sometimes people may get hurt or die, but life is full of risks. All of us must live or die with the decisions that we make."

Galin nodded. "Yes, you will."

Artis blinked. "Will? Will what? It's no secret, but

you aren't going to survive long enough to see the next sunset."

Galin glared at him.

"But, your friends don't have to join you," Artis said with a smile.

Galin's ears perked up. "Go on."

"I need a few pieces of information, that's all."

Was he asking Galin to betray Brock, Mae, and the rest of his followers in the mountains? Yes, that had to be it. He couldn't. No, he wouldn't. Maybe he could get information from Artis. Perhaps. Would it hurt to try? Galin smiled. "What do you want to know?"

Artis grinned. "I didn't know you'd be that easy. Well, okay. Where are your forces?"

If Galin gave that information too quickly, Artis would be suspicious, right? "I can't tell you that."

Artis put on a knight's steel gauntlet on his right hand. "I think you will."

Galin's eyes widened, staring at the gauntlet. "Please, ask me something else. My father is with them."

"Your father is dead. He has been dead a long time now." Artis' face lit up. "Ahh, the blacksmith. Well, if you value his life more than those of your friends, I guess you've made your decision." He looked towards the door. "Guards!"

The door flew open and both guards had their swords at the ready.

"No, wait! I'll tell you, but please leave Ellis and Jena alone. Let them go and I'll tell you anything," Galin cried. Was he convincing him? Could Artis be that foolish? Galin held back a smile as Artis closed the door.

Artis leaned in. "Well?"

"They're in Qrento. We came through the Wailing Mountains on an old mountain trail where my adoptive father used to take us hunting." He turned and secretly poked himself in the eye. Tears flowed down his cheeks. "Don't hurt them, please don't."

"What was your next move?"

Galin scowled at Artis. "We were going to liberate Drusas from you!"

Artis nodded. "If we send forces down to Qrento, we'd find them and stop your invasion?"

Galin tore his eyes away from Artis. "Yes."

"I see." Artis opened the cell door again. There was a man pushing a small cart with an iron bowl filled with burning embers and iron pokers buried in the fire. The bald man was enormous. He was taller than Artis, and his arms were larger than Galin's thighs. "Albert, do you believe him?"

Albert gave Galin a toothless smile. "No." He tore off Galin's shirt, exposing his chest.

Artis nodded. "Me either." He pulled out a poker and its end was glowing red. He grinned at Galin. "Shall we start again?" He pressed the hot iron poker against his chest.

Galin screamed.

CHAPTER 21

Volunteers

Galin cradled his broken right arm as they tossed him inside the dark cell, slamming the door shut. He grasped the dirt floor. Galin struggled to sit up, but got nowhere. The room was blurry and his head was spinning. What was happening to him?

A soft pair of hands helped Galin lean against the wall. "Are you all right?"

Galin could only manage a grunt.

Jena kissed his forehead. "It's all right, my love. I've got you." She touched his arm and bowed her head.

He struggled to keep his eyes open. He could see Jena's mouth speak the incantation, but couldn't hear it. He blinked. A warm sensation flowed over his arm and his mind began to clear.

Jena screamed as her right arm broke in two with a shard of bone sticking out of her forearm. She recoiled into a small ball, praying to Odella. A moment later, a soft light came over her. She rubbed her forearm as she slid next to Galin. "Feeling better?"

"Why do you do that to yourself?" Galin asked. He already knew the answer, but he always had to ask. Why would anyone take on the injuries of others and hope the mighty Odella would heal them? Nuts.

Jena smiled. "I can't bear to have you hurt. After all, we still have to get married."

"You can forget that crap, Jena," Ellis said. "Didn't you tell him?"

Galin looked blankly at Jena. "Tell me what?"

Jena kissed him. "Don't worry about it. It's not like we can do anything about it."

"About what?" Galin demanded.

"They're going to hang us at first light," Jena said.

"All of us? Not you and Ellis."

Ellis nodded. "All of us."

"They promised you wouldn't be harmed! Damn him!" Galin yelled.

"Who?" Jena asked.

"Artis the Black. He promised to let you two go if I didn't use my dragon magic."

Jena blinked. "How does he know about that?"

Ellis looked way. Tears started to flow down his cheeks. "I...I couldn't help it. It hurt so bad."

Galin's face softened. "I understand. But we still have to figure out what to do."

"What about using your powers to get us out?" Jena asked.

"I'm not a mage. I need my sword to do that."

"What about burning the ropes?" Ellis asked. "Like when we were captured by the goblins."

"There was only one goblin awake and you two kept him busy." Galin shook his head. "I don't know. I just don't know."

WHEN THE SUNLIGHT crept through the window, the cell door burst open. Six men swarmed around Galin, Ellis, and Jena and threw black hoods over their heads. Galin felt iron shackles clamp onto his wrists and feet. "What's this?"

"Don't want you to burn through the ropes now, do we?" a man's voice said.

"Did you really think we weren't listening last night?" another said.

They hoisted Galin up by his shoulders and dragged him out of the cell.

Galin felt his feet dragging along a stone floor. The tips of his boots were sliding over the seams in between the stones. They hadn't gone outside yet. Yeah, they had a chance if he could get out of these chains. Their only chance was to get free before they got outside. What about Jena? There were worse things they could to do her than hanging her if he got out, but failed. What would they do to her? Just because Artis the Black was not a man of his word about freeing them, would he be about hurting them? Screw it! He willed his rage to surface. The tingling came from his heart and spread throughout his body.

"Damn it," a man said. "His skin's getting hot to the touch."

"He's using his dragon magic," Artis said. "Quick, knock him out!"

Artis? He was here, too. Galin tried to pull his wrists out of the shackles. A blunt object slammed into the back of his head, knocking him to the ground. His world went black.

GALIN JUMPED as ice-cold water splashed over his face. The morning sun warmed his back. He looked around. There was a newly constructed gallows in the market square, and he and his friends were its first customers. He felt the coarse rope around his neck as the executioner hoisted him up. His mouth was stuffed with a dirty rag from the stables. His hands were shackled behind his back and his feet were chained close together. Even if he managed to burn the ropes, he couldn't do anything. How disappointed the Dark Elves would be when they found out that the human they feared the most had died at the hands of a traitor.

On a small platform, in front of the gallows, stood Artis the Black and his assistant, Lena. A ring of towns-folk stretched from one side of the platform, all the way around the gallows, until it reached the platform again. Galin saw the glee on Artis' face. *That bastard won!*

Artis held up his hands. "Good morning, citizens of

Drusas. Today, I bring you grave news about a terrible deed." He pointed at Galin, Ellis, and Jena. "Those three were planning to attack Drusas, killing you and your families." A crack of a smile made its way through that fake, stoic face. "As governor, I cannot allow such a betrayal to our glorious city, to you, and to our gracious rulers, the Darkstriders."

Galin looked around. No one was joyful at Artis' announcement; in fact, their faces grew redder. Were they going to be helped by the people?

The black-hooded executioner stood next to a tall lever, which would release the trapdoors under their feet at the far end of the gallows.

Artis raised his hands in the air. "My friends, today we celebrate a way forward in our new reality. With their deaths, we will prove to our rulers that we do not need their orcs to come down from the keep. Instead, let us prosper together." He nodded to the executioner.

Galin stared at the hooded man, who just stood there. His grip on the lever was tightening, but he didn't pull it.

Artis glared at the executioner. "Well? What the hell are you waiting for? Do it! Do it, now!"

"Don't do it, Phil," Karl said as he pushed his way through the crowd.

Artis blinked. "Sheriff? What are you doing?"

"It's over, Artis. Your reign is finished."

Galin looked behind the sheriff. The crowd started to follow him towards the platform. Lena stepped back, only to be blocked by the crowd encircling the platform.

Artis shook his head. "No, you can't do this. I am the governor!"

"No, you're the murderer those bastards put in charge," Karl retorted. "Everyone here lost someone to your greed and lust for power. I'll kill you!" Karl charged at the platform.

Artis glanced back at the five guards, still loyal to him, blocking the people from getting on the platform. He grabbed Lena by the arm. "I didn't do it alone. She was the brains behind it all!" He threw Lena off the platform into the crowd of people. He disappeared behind the guards.

Lena jumped to her feet. "I told him not to hurt anyone. I told him not to steal from the nobles!" Her face went pale as the people took knives and short swords from underneath their garments. "I tried to save you! But, he didn't listen." She spun around again and again and again to face the advancing threat. The circle grew smaller as the vengeance-seeking towns-folk got closer. Tears flowed down her face. "I'm sorry!" she screamed.

Galin turned his head as his bloodthirsty saviors savagely killed her. After a few moments, there was nothing but silence. He looked towards the platform. There was a heap of flesh and blood that used to be Lena Blunt. How long had they been holding back their vengeance from their persecutors?

"Cut them down," Karl said.

Jena took one look at Lena's body and threw up over the side of the gallows.

Ellis didn't even look at it.

"Was that really necessary?" Galin asked. "That was…barbaric."

Karl waved his hand. "That was none of your concern, sire."

Galin blinked.

"We've decided to join you."

"What about the guards?" another shouted.

Karl walked towards the five guards being held by the crowd. "Hmm. Kill them."

"No! Don't do it!" Galin yelled. "I will not let my kingdom be reborn under such barbarism." He walked over to the guards. "You saw what they did to Lena?"

They nodded.

"Do you want that to happen to you?"

They all shook their heads no.

Galin smiled. "Good. Start off by telling us, where is Artis the Black."

"He ran to Iron Fist Keep, to get help," a guard said.

"Will you join us? It's either that or I'll give you over to them."

Without hesitation, they all nodded.

Galin looked at Karl. "I'll let you handle them."

"What now?" Karl asked.

Galin looked around. They were all looking to him as if he was already crowned king. "Who is coming with us to infiltrate Iron Fist Keep?"

"Abby and I will go," Karl said.

"What about the rest of us?" a voice yelled from the crowd. "How can we help?"

"We have a few old knights who fought under your father in Drusas. They agreed to help you, and our people are thirsty for Darkstrider blood," Karl said.

Galin looked over at the bloody pile of flesh that used to be Lena Blunt. "I see that." His eyes focused on Karl. "I want them to start a riot near the keep, but outside of arrow range."

Karl nodded. "To draw them out?"

"Yes, the fewer orcs we have to fight inside, the better. By the time they come back from addressing the riot, we'll be in position to ambush them."

"What about the governor?" Ellis asked. "Surely, he's going to warn them."

Galin swallowed. "Maybe, but that's a risk we have to take." Galin extended his hand to Karl. "Glad to have you with us."

Karl shook it vigorously. "You've got no idea how long we've been waiting for your arrival, sire."

Ellis grinned. "Let's kick some orc ass!"

TASAR WAS in a small room next to the gatehouse in Iron Fist Keep. The walls were made of granite and the two windows were barred. He sat on a simple bed, rubbing the end of his right leg. Sure, the peg leg helped him get around, but the constant rubbing made his skin raw. He looked up as someone banged on the door. "Enter."

A Feral Orc captain with two axes hanging from its belt opened the door. The bald orc had enormous arms and its skin was more gray than green.

Tasar rolled his eyes. "What do you want, Gul?"

Gul smiled. "An old friend is here to see you."

"Who?"

"Artis the Black."

Tasar put his peg leg back on and grinned. "I can't wait to see him."

He followed Gul downstairs and outside the gate. On the drawbridge stood Artis the Black. Tasar looked down at the moat. Molten rock flowed around Iron Fist Keep as if it was a volcano. Perfect! "What can we do for you, Governor?"

Artis' shirt was soaked with sweat. His breaths were shallow and short. "I-I ran here all the way from Drusas. There's-there's been a revolt."

Tasar raised an eyebrow. "Really?"

"What revolt?" Gul demanded.

Tasar raised his hand, silencing the Feral Orc. "All in good time, my friend."

Artis blinked. "Why is he listening to you? Did you join the Darkstriders, again?"

"Let's just say that we have…mutual goals." His eyes narrowed and his face hardened. "Why are you here and not fighting the revolt as we speak?"

Artis stepped back. The blood drained from his face. "I need help to retake the town."

Tasar stroked his cheek. "I'd like to help you, but there's a matter of the money you stole from me."

"I'm sorry. I barely got away with my life. I wasn't able to get my chests from the vault." His lips began to tremble when he saw Gul cross his arms.

"Well, that's a shame," Tasar said as he walked next

to Artis, who kept staring at Gul. "What are they planning to do?"

"I-I'm not sure." Artis looked around as if the answer was lying on the ground beneath him. "I-I think they're going to attack Iron Fist Keep."

Gul yanked Artis by the shirt, hoisting him up in the air. "When? How do they plan to attack us? Tell me!"

Tasar shook his head. "Tsk, tsk, tsk. Gul, can't you see he's scared?" He leaned closer to Artis. "I'd tell him before he gets…antsy."

Sweat poured down Artis' face as he stared into the orc's eyes. "They have an army in the mountains and they were seeking volunteers in Drusas. The-the boy uses dragon magic."

"How'd you manage to capture him?" Gul asked.

"We threatened his fiancée," Artis replied.

"I see." Tasar rubbed his chin. "So, why would they attack the keep that way? They must know if they put Iron Fist Keep under siege, reinforcements will come." He glared at Artis. "Can you explain that?"

Artis nodded. "Yes, they were looking for people who were familiar with the inside of the keep, so they could open the gate for their army to run inside."

"What about the traitors from Drusas? What will they be doing?" Gul demanded as he shook Artis. "Tell me, damn it!"

Tasar smiled. "You'd better tell him."

"I don't know! I really don't know," Artis sobbed.

Tasar watched the yellow stream run down Artis'

leg, forming a pool of urine beneath him. "For some reason, I believe him."

Artis tried to smile. "You see," he said to Gul, "I can help you."

"Do we really need him?" Gul asked Tasar.

Tasar waved his hand. "I'm good." His dark, sunken eyes narrowed. "How about you, governor?"

Artis shook his head. "No, I can help you. Please."

Tasar pointed at Gul's feet. "I think he pissed on your shoes."

Gul looked down. The urine puddle settled around his leather boots. "Damn humans!" He tossed Artis off the drawbridge. His screams stopped as he was swallowed by the molten rock. Gul stared at the moat for another moment. "Suggestions?"

"Yes, we stop them from raising the gate."

"How?"

Tasar grinned. "We catch their scouts that try to sneak inside."

"What about the town?"

"Who cares? The more pressing matter is the army in the mountains." Tasar looked up at Gul. "Send a rider west to Staerdale Castle and let them know what is happening. If this uprising gets a hold of this keep, it will take a lot of Darkstriders to get them out, maybe even making the kingdom vulnerable elsewhere."

Grul looked beyond the drawbridge, towards Drusas. "Very well. If I was them, I'd try to draw us out, to thin out our ranks."

Tasar nodded. "Sounds…logical. May I send a letter with your rider?"

"Who's it for?"

"My daughter, Chalia. She's joined your ranks, just like her mother, Beldroth."

Gul smiled. "I fought with Beldroth. She was an amazing pyromancer."

"The best," Tasar said. Both Tasar and Gul hurried inside.

Attack

After darkness fell over Drusas, Galin, Jena, Ellis, Karl, and Abby rode the small trail up the mountain, north of Iron Fist Keep. Riding up the steep mountains towards their camp seemed to take twice as long.

"How many soldiers do you have?" Karl asked.

"Over five hundred," Galin said. "My father and my general are training them now."

"Mae's a general?" Ellis sniffed. "You never even bothered to ask me."

Jena smacked Ellis in the back of the head. "Knock it off, Ellis."

"I thought your father was dead," Abby noted.

Galin nodded. "I never met my real father. The only father I ever knew was Brock Feran. He was the king's blacksmith. He and his wife, Sally, snuck me out of Staerdale Castle before it fell, when I was just a baby." He patted Thea. "My horse is named after the one person who not only saved me but saved the future of Axain. Her name was Thea the Loyal. If we win this, she will be remembered as the bravest knight who ever lived."

Karl blinked. "She?"

"Yes, she was the only female knight in the kingdom of Axain. But in the end, she was the bravest." Galin pointed at the firelight just beyond the rise. "We're here."

It was like a hero coming home after a long and treacherous quest. As Galin rode into camp, he was swarmed by Brock, Mae, and the rest of his soldiers. As Galin dismounted, they moved away from him.

Brock smiled from ear to ear. "Glad you're back, son." He hugged Galin.

"Did we get more people?" Ellis asked as he jumped down from Runt.

Mae nodded. "Yes, we got another two hundred." Her eyes followed Ellis as he approached her.

"Where'd they come from?" Jena asked.

"We ambushed a few Darkstrider patrols. When we were searching for more, we came across a caravan of warriors looking to join the fight," Brock said. "Once we were certain that they were okay, we brought them here."

Galin leaned in close to Brock's ear. "Are you certain they are not Dark Elves?"

Brock opened his mouth.

"I am certain, young Galin," a short male elf said as he broke through the crowd. His ghastly looking skin told the world his age. He wore the red robes of a war mage.

Galin's face lit up. "Nyna!" He ran over to give his old teacher a hug, but his old teacher pushed him back.

"That's not very kingly, young prince," Nyna said. "Dark Elves pretending to be humans are pretty easy to find, if you know what to look for."

"Do you have any other war mages with you?"

Nyna shook his head. "No, but I did get word from the Shadow Mage. She will join us once we attack Staerdale Castle, but not before."

Brock sighed. "We're a long way from that."

"It doesn't matter. First things first." Galin smiled. "Here's what we're going to do…"

As the early morning sun yawned over the horizon, Galin smiled. His army had moved into position over night, just out of sight of Iron Fist Keep. The soldiers were anxious, ready, and scared. Sure, the training Brock and Mae gave them helped to alleviate some of their anxiety, but nothing prepares one for combat more than combat itself.

Galin swallowed. This was it. This day would be the first day that all those people who died to keep him alive would begin to be avenged. He only knew a couple, but Brock told him that it was hundreds who had sacrificed themselves to give him this chance to take back the kingdom and free his people. Did he really believe in the Dark Elf prophecy? No, but they did. Once word got out about Iron Fist Keep, win or lose, the Darkstriders would send everything they had against them, right? Yeah, probably. Galin looked over at Jena. He would marry her before the sun went down that night.

Ellis tapped Galin on the shoulder. "Ready?"

Galin nodded. "Whoever thought that three derelict kids from Crey Village would be doing this?"

"Not me." Ellis pointed at the cart near the road. Karl and Abby were dressed like farmers, sitting at the front of the cart. Karl had the reins in his left hand, staring at Galin as if anxious to get started. Jena was already crawling underneath a few bales of hay. "Our rides ready."

"Let's go." Galin and Ellis climbed into the back of the cart with Jena, hidden from view underneath the hay. He winced as they piled on bale after bale of hay. *This is going to be fun.*

The minutes seemed like hours to Galin hidden underneath the bales of hay. He felt every bump, rock, and divot in the road leading to Iron Fist Keep. He started to move a bale of hay.

Ellis grabbed Galin by the shoulder. "Hey, are you trying to get us caught?"

Without saying a word, Galin threw him off. He only moved it enough to peer out the front of the cart. His opening was just below the bench that Karl and Abby sat on in the front of the cart. Beyond the horse, he saw Iron Fist Keep. He didn't focus on the large tower, rather the drawbridge and the portcullis. The moat was between ten and fifteen feet wide, with lava running through it. It couldn't be natural because there were no active volcanoes, right? Yeah, it had to be magic. Perhaps a pyromancer create it. The drawbridge looked worn and in need of repair. Six Feral Orcs with swords in their sheaths stood at the end of the draw-bridge on the outside of the moat.

Karl slowed the cart down as the Feral Orcs blocked the drawbridge.

"What's your business here, human?" the largest Feral Orc asked.

Galin's stomach twisted. If things went wrong, being buried underneath all this hay, he was in no posi-tion to react. Their lives depended on Karl and Abby.

"I'm the sheriff of Drusas. I just got back from Fison." Karl looked around. "Are you expecting trou-ble? Maybe I could help."

The orc walked behind the cart. "What are you hauling?"

Karl laughed.

Galin's eyes widened as the Feral Orc raced back towards the front and glared at Karl.

"Why are you laughing at me, human?" he demanded.

Karl pointed at the bales of hay in the back. "Are you telling me that you don't know what hay looks like?" He laughed some more.

The Feral Orc heard more laughing behind him. He whirled around to see the five other orcs joining with Karl. "Of course I know it's hay. But, I still have to check." He walked behind the cart and unsheathed his sword.

Karl's laughter fell off his face.

Galin motioned Jena and Ellis to pull their feet towards the front. Ellis ignored him.

The orc thrust his sword into the bales.

The tip of the blade broke into their hiding place and right between Ellis' legs. Ellis wanted to scream, but Galin clamped his hand over Ellis' mouth.

The Feral Orc pulled out the sword. "You're right. It's just hay."

"I told you," Karl said.

"There's been a rebellion in Drusas, Sheriff. Please, quickly move through the keep. The commander ordered the keep to be sealed off today."

"Why's that?"

The orc grunted. "They expect the humans to attack."

"I'll be quick," Karl said as he cracked the reins, hurrying the horses pulling the cart inside the keep.

Galin peered out through the small hole between the bales of hay. He felt no heat radiating from the lava flowing through the moat as they crossed the drawbridge. Yeah, it was definitely magical.

The courtyard was enormous. It was much bigger inside the walls than it appeared from the outside. The ground was littered with broken furniture and haystacks. The stone wall around the well in the center of the courtyard was in pieces. His nose wrinkled as a formation of Feral Orcs passed in front of the cart.

"What's this?" Gul demanded as he grabbed the

horse's bridle, stopping the cart. His eyes flared at the orc escorting the cart through the keep. "No one was to be admitted inside the keep. Why are they here? Answer me!"

Galin blinked as he saw Gul grab one of his axes and throw it at the orc.

Gul smiled as the orc crashed to the ground. His eyes narrowed and his face hardened. "What are you doing here, human?"

"I-I-I'm sorry, sir," Karl said. "We are just on our way to Drusas. That's all."

"Will you let us pass?" Abby asked.

Gul frowned. "Did you check the cart already?" he asked another orc.

"Yes, Commander," it said.

Gul passed the bridle over to the orc. "Hold this." He walked around the back of the cart.

Galin held his breath. He couldn't see Gul, but he felt him climb onto the cart. He heard Gul toss a bale of hay out of the cart. Any moment now, they'd be uncovered. If they moved too soon, they risked Brock and Mae not being ready to swarm through the gate.

Gul tossed another bale on the ground.

Galin's heart stopped as sunlight penetrated their hiding place. He nodded to Jena and Ellis, signaling them to be ready. He willed anger and rage to the forefront of his mind. Reliving Sally's death over and over in his mind conjured that familiar tingle in his heart. It spread throughout his body. Tiny arcs began jumping across his skin. Galin grabbed his sword. As his hand touched the hilt, the arcs jumped from his skin to the sword and it started to glow.

Gul hoisted the bale of hay right over Galin and looked into his eyes. "Damn it!" He thrust the bale into Galin's chest, pinning him to the cart. "It's them!"

Ellis kicked Gul's right ankle, knocking him off the cart. He threw a bale at Gul. With a dagger in each hand, Ellis leaped off the cart.

Galin's eyes were glowing before he hit the ground. *Offense, think offense.*

Karl pulled his sword out from underneath his seat and jumped off the cart, moving closer to Galin.

Abby pulled cedar chips out from her spell components bag.

With her short sword drawn, Jena jumped off the cart, ready to face the Darkstriders with Galin.

"Get them!" Gul yelled as he ran towards the gatehouse.

Feral Orcs flowed out of the tower like a rushing river. Galin swallowed. Was this a mistake? Would he get Jena killed?

"Galin!" Ellis screamed. "Which way?"

"The gate!" Galin charged two Feral Orcs, rushing them from the gate. He screamed as his legs did a split in midair and he swung his glowing sword parallel to the ground. The hot blade sliced through their legs, just below the knee.

Another orc, with its great ax raised, charged at Ellis.

"At least I can kill this thing." Ellis threw his dagger

and skewered its left eye. He leaped on top of the blinded orc and slit its throat with his other dagger.

Abby faced the orcs coming out of the tower with the cedar chips in her hands. She never took her eyes off her targets. Her mouth uttered an inaudible incantation. Five fire bolts appeared in front of her.

The orcs stopped, as if they recognized the spell, and ran for cover.

They were too late. The fire bolts raced across the courtyard and exploded when they struck their targets.

Karl decapitated a Feral Orc and rushed next to Galin. "The gate controls are in the gatehouse, just to the right of it." He raced towards the open door.

"Wait!" Galin yelled, only a few steps behind him. "Ellis, Abby, stay out here and cover our backs. Jena, tell Brock it's now or never."

"But…"

"Go!" Without waiting for a response, Galin rushed inside the gatehouse after Karl.

Karl screamed as Gul slammed his ax into Karl's chest.

Galin charged the orc leader, but he didn't notice the dead orc and he tripped over it, crashing onto the wooden floor.

Gul laughed. He raised his ax above Galin's head. "Some prophecy." With all his might, he brought down his ax like a guillotine.

Galin rolled to the right.

Gul's ax slammed into the wooden floor. He yanked on it, but it wouldn't come out.

Galin thrust his sword into Gul's chest.

The orc screamed and then slumped to the floor.

Karl pointed at the iron gate controls along the wall. "If…if you break the handle and smash the gears, they won't be able to raise the drawbridge nor lower the portcullis."

Galin nodded. Summoning up all his power, he grasped the iron gears. That smell of scorching flesh invaded his nostrils. He looked down. His hands were burning, not by an enemy or a fire, but by his own power. He had to calm down. The iron gears began to glow. He had to hold on, just long enough to seize the gears. Galin felt his skin begin to bubble. He screamed.

"What is—" Abby's eyes welled up as she knelt down next to her dying husband.

The glowing gears began to melt. They melded together. No one, save by magic, could ever close those gates again. Galin lowered his head, expelling the rage from his mind. As he calmed down, the dragon magic left his body. Galin looked at his forearms. They were blistered and burnt. *Karl!* "I'm sorry."

Abby was sobbing on Karl's chest. "He's dead!"

"We have to go." He grabbed her by the arm.

"No! I want to stay," Abby said as she yanked her arm from his grasp.

Galin yanked her up. "We've got to go. Now!"

She looked down at her dead, loving husband.

"Would he want you to die here? Right now? Or would he want you to fight on?"

Abby opened her mouth, but nothing came out.

"Would he?" Galin demanded.

"No! No, he…wouldn't."

"Come on." Galin sprinted out of the gatehouse.

Ellis yanked his daggers out of another orc.

"It's done," Galin said.

Ellis grinned. "About time you came out here."

Galin tightened his grip on his sword. His heart pounded in his throat as sixty orcs bore down on them.

Iron Fist Keep

"This sucks!" Ellis yelled.

Galin stared at the smiling Feral Orcs advancing on them. Two versus sixty? He created visions of Jena being tossed to a horde of wild wolves, enraging his heart with vengeance. The tingling sensation spread throughout his body like a virus. His skin was littered with tiny electrical arcs, not too dissimilar from lightning, only smaller.

The orcs stopped, unsure about what was happening to Galin. They moved to Galin's flank, blocking them from escaping out the gate.

"Where's our pyromancer? We could use her about now."

Galin shook his head. "It's just—"

"I'm here," Abby said as she sat in the doorway. "Just keep them off me for ten seconds."

"You only live once." Ellis whipped a dagger at the closest orc. It hit its mark and pierced the beast's heart. He snatched the dagger from its chest.

Abby piled seven cedar chips on the ground in front of her. She stared at the oncoming Feral Orcs. "Den nrad nier."

Several orcs armed with axes charged Galin.

With his eyes glowing, he drew the orcs away from Abby. Galin thrust his sword into the belly of one.

Another orc swung his ax to take his head clean off his shoulder.

Galin ducked and rammed his shoulder into its chest, knocking the wind out of it.

"Den nrad nier," Abby said in a trance-like state.

The orcs jumped back.

Galin looked up. A cloud began to form over the courtyard. It was not white, but red. Red, like the embers in a fire. "Get back!" Galin yelled as he yanked Ellis towards the gatehouse.

"Wizard! Take cover!" Tasar yelled from the entrance to the tower.

The orcs scattered.

"Den nrad nier." Abby's eyes followed the orcs as they ran for shelter.

A single fireball appeared high above the courtyard. It crashed to the ground, exploding on impact. Three orcs burst into flames. Another fireball appeared, then another, then another. The raining fireballs exploded, setting fire to everything. Several orcs hid behind a haystack; they didn't make it.

Galin and Ellis ran inside the gatehouse, right behind Abby. "This is awesome!" Ellis said.

Galin's eyes watched in awe of Abby's display of power. "With magic, there's always a cost."

Abby screamed and collapsed to the ground.

The cloud disappeared and the fireballs stopped falling from the sky.

Ellis wrinkled his nose. "What's that smell? Barbecued orc?"

"Come on!" Galin charged into the courtyard with his sword at the ready.

"Attack!" Tasar screamed as he took his position behind the oncoming wave of orcs.

The mass of orcs charged towards Galin and Ellis. He looked over at his friend. "I'm sorry."

Ellis grinned. "No you're not." He charged at one orc while throwing a dagger at another. Both went down hard.

Galin bowled over three orcs and decapitated another. He turned his head toward the thunderous sound of mounted riders racing over the wooden drawbridge and into the courtyard. Brock had arrived.

Brock leaped from his horse, knocking down one orc and cutting the arm off another. "Mae will be here in a minute! We need to hold the drawbridge."

Three fire bolts appeared above Galin's head. He ducked and they crashed harmlessly into the ground. "Ellis, grab Abby!" They formed a semicircle around the gate, fighting off the onslaught of Feral Orcs.

Galin's infantry, led by Mae, charged over the bridge. They poured into the courtyard with such ferocity that Tasar ran into the tower. They outnumbered the orcs many times to one.

"Tasar's getting away!" Jena yelled as she joined Galin. "Let's get him!"

"No," Galin said as he severed an arm off an orc. "You're needed here. I'll go." He fought his way through the sea of fighting humans and orcs towards the tower. Two orcs charged Galin from inside the tower as he approached the entrance. He swung his sword at one, taking its head clean off.

The other orc swung its ax.

Pain shot through Galin's left leg. He thrust his sword into the orc's chest. Galin felt a warm fluid running down his leg. He looked down. Blood. He was bleeding. The ax must have nicked his left thigh. He ran inside, button-hooked around the door and leaned against the wall. "Great." He tore a piece of his shirt and tied it around his leg. Sure, it wasn't bad, but he wasn't at full strength, either. All that mattered now was to get Tasar.

He looked around. The room was empty save a broken desk and chair in the corner. On the far side of the room was a staircase. The stairs hugged the wall and were no more than three feet wide. There was no banister or anything to stop someone from falling. *This is it.* Galin bolted up the stairs.

"Get him!" Tasar yelled above Galin.

Orcs! There had to be orcs with him. Galin gripped his sword even tighter. If he rushed too much, he would deliver his head to Tasar and his orcs. If he moved too slowly, Tasar would get away. Did he care about those Tasar would leave behind? No, he was an assassin, after all. He had to get to Tasar. Already up two floors, Galin pressed forward towards the third.

Three orcs charged down the stairs in a single line with their axes raised. The first one swung at Galin's head.

He ducked. He kicked the orc's feet out from underneath him.

The orc screamed as it fell two floors and crashed into a broken chair. A chair leg pierced through its chest.

Pain shot through Galin's leg. He thrust his glowing sword at the second orc, the third orc close behind, skewering both through the heart. He yanked his sword from their bodies as they fell. He looked down at his leg. His leg was bleeding even more now. Light-headed, he was feeling light…headed. Blood, he was losing too much blood. He didn't have a lot of time. Galin looked up. The door to the roof. *Tasar must be up there!*

Galin burst through the door.

Tasar didn't even look up. "Dit onska ni jeg." A bright light appeared in front of him. Bexon's Dimensional Tunnel was beginning to form.

"No you don't!" Galin charged Tasar, knocking him to the ground.

Tasar cursed as the light disappeared. "Damn you!" He pulled a dagger from underneath his robes and lunged at Galin.

Galin knocked away Tasar's dagger.

Tasar kicked Galin in the leg, opening his wound even more.

The pain shot through his body. His leg collapsed underneath him. Galin dropped his sword.

Tasar smiled as he picked it up. "I believe you owe me a leg, but I'll take your head instead." He raised the sword.

Faint, he felt so…faint. Warm blood spilled out his leg. Spots. More and more black spots appeared in front of his eyes. This was the end.

"Leave my husband alone!" Jena screamed as she charged Tasar.

"What?" Tasar turned towards her.

Jena swung her short sword, cutting off the hand holding Galin's sword. She recoiled to deliver the fatal blow.

Galin's sword fell to the ground.

Tasar moved to the edge. He pulled out a cedar chip and his mouth spoke an inaudible word.

Six fire bolts appeared by Tasar's head.

"No!" Galin grabbed his sword and severed Tasar's peg leg.

Jena thrust her short sword at Tasar's chest. She missed.

Tasar crashed to the ground. His fearful eyes looked up at Jena. "Please, don't. I have a daughter."

Jena raised her sword. "So did my mother!"

Tasar rolled even closer to the edge to avoid her blade.

Galin kicked Tasar, pushing him over the edge.

Tasar screamed, and then was silent.

Galin crawled over to the edge. Tasar had fallen three stories into the courtyard. Now, his body was just one amongst dozens of humans and orcs. He rolled onto his back. "I…I'm dying."

Jena pulled him from the edge with tears streaming down her face. "Not if I have anything to say about it. Don't give up on me, damn it!"

Blackness. Spots. Cold. Galin saw Jena prepare to heal him. "No, don't. I…I'm too far gone. It'll kill you."

"No, I can't live without you. I…I have to do this." She wiped the tears from her eyes.

Galin started to cry. "Please, don't. I love you too much."

She bent down and kissed his forehead. "I love you. I'm with you in this life and the next."

"I…I—" Darkness overtook Galin. A few minutes later, he jumped up. Jena! She was laying on the floor next to him. Her blood was spilled out onto the roof. He sobbed on her chest. "Why did you do that? I can't…can't be without you." He stared up at the sky. "Odella, give her back to me!" He collapsed over her.

"I-I love you, Galin," Jena whispered.

He hugged her. "You're okay?"

She smiled. "You were *almost* too far gone."

Galin's army cheered in the courtyard.

"I guess we won," Galin said.

Jena sat up and kissed him. "You've got a promise to keep."

He passionately kissed her. "I do."

· · ·

TEN MINUTES LATER, Galin and Jena emerged from the tower. Brock and Mae were in front of the formation.

"We've won," Brock said.

"The last few orcs surrendered," Mae said. "What shall we do with them?"

"Kill them!" a voice yelled from the back of the formation.

"They can't be trusted," Brock added.

Galin and Jena moved to the right of the formation, right across courtyard to where Tasar had fallen. Two dozen Feral Orcs were guarded by his soldiers. This was his first real call as king. What kind of kingdom did he want? One built on vengeance or one built on freedom? "Who is senior amongst you?"

A female orc stepped forward. She was strong and well-muscled. Her face was feminine and her chest was not too dissimilar from a human woman. "I am. Lieutenant Yotul."

"What are we to do with you?"

She laughed. "Why are you asking? We know you're going to kill us."

Was he? Galin's stomach kept twisting. Killing in battle was one thing, but executing them now would be...*murder*. Was he a murderer? No, he wasn't. "What happens to you if you go back?"

Yotul looked away. "The same thing. At least you won't torture us as badly. Tanyl will hand us over to the seers for questioning. No one survives that."

"So, you're better off not going back. Is that what you're saying?"

Brock grabbed Galin's shoulder. "What are you doing?"

Galin pulled away. "The right thing." He looked back at Yotul. "We are not murderers. I won't kill you. There is no honor in executing soldiers who, because of where they were born, are fighting on the other side. No, I won't do that."

Brock frowned.

"Do you know what freedom is?"

Yotul shook her head. "No."

"It is when you can wake up every morning and decide your own destiny, not relying on someone to give you orders. We fight to give our children a better life."

Yotul looked away. "I never knew…freedom before. When I have children, I want them to have a better life, too."

Galin smiled. "Yes, every human, Vulwin Elf, Feral Orc, Dwarf, and Gnome all want a better life and the freedom to pursue it." He untied her hands. "I'm letting you go."

Fear fell over Yotul's face. "No, we can't. They'll kill us."

"Galin, stop this madness," Brock said.

Galin glared at him. "No. This is the right thing to do."

"Thank you," Yotul said. "But, Feral Orcs live to fight for honor, and I'm sure your people would not welcome us after what we've done."

She was right and Galin knew it. "I welcome you. If

you swear allegiance to my army and help us defeat the Darkstriders, I will welcome you in our ranks."

"All right." Yotul got down on one knee and the other orcs did the same. "We swear to follow you and defeat the enemies of freedom so all of us can share in its bounty."

Galin smiled. "Rise, my friends." He held Jena's hand.

Her face was glowing. "Time to keep your promise." She kissed him.

A bright light flashed across the courtyard.

Galin whirled around. "What was that?"

A few soldiers rushed over. "The Dark Elf, he's gone."

Jena pulled Galin's angered face towards her. "Forget him. We're too busy."

Galin smiled. "You're right. Let's get married." They passionately kissed and the crowd cheered.

CHAPTER 24

Only the Beginning

Kade Ravenward used to be a knight, but that was before he killed his brother the king, Galin IV of Ravenward. His once powerful arms had turned flabby and his chiseled stomach became round. He was a mere shadow of what he used to be. When he took Tanyl's offer to become king, he had no idea how little power he would actually have. Kade was a mere puppet of the Darkstriders and he knew it. He pushed through the double doors into the Great Hall.

"Thank you for your report, Tasar," a tall Dark Elf with short, black hair wearing purple robes said as he kicked Tasar's head across the floor.

"Bad day, Tanyl?" Kade asked. "You are going to clean that up, aren't you?"

Tanyl glared at him. "Your nephew just took Iron Fist Keep."

Kade stopped in mid-stride towards the throne. "What?" he asked as he sat down. "How is that possible?"

"And some of the Feral Orcs joined him." Tanyl started to pace across the floor. "Now, they control everything east of the Wailing Mountains. I never saw this coming."

Kade grinned. "When am I going to see your head roll across the floor?"

"Only after yours."

"What now?"

Tanyl rubbed his chin. "No more worrying about a rebellion, it's already started."

"You want to take the keep back?"

"Yes, that's the key to securing Axain, you dolt!" Tanyl sniffed. "You were never the bright one, Kade. All the brains went into your brother."

Kade tightened his fist.

Tanyl waved him towards the door. "Go and get the Feral Orc regiment commanders."

"I'm not your servant!"

Tanyl smiled. "Yes you are. Now, go!"

Kade frowned as he moved towards the door. He'd orchestrated the death of his family, for what? He had more power when Galin IV was king. Maybe he could set things right. Maybe his sins towards his people could be forgiven. He longed to walk into a tavern without heads turning away. Just to walk down the road within the castle walls without people turning their backs to him would be worth more than the throne. Kade never thought that being a king would be so, lonely. He turned back to Tanyl. "What if he wins? What happens to you?"

Tanyl scowled. "He won't."

I've never seen him so scared, Kade thought as he left the Great Hall.

A FEW DAYS LATER, the courtyard transformed into a beautiful oasis in the Wailing Mountains. The haystacks were in the corners. The front of the tower was clean and was fit for royalty to live in.

On the steps going into the tower stood a priestess of Odella, with Galin and Jena standing below her. Flowers decorated the steps, and the audience from both his army and the citizens of Drusas looked on.

Galin held Jena's hand. "With this ring, I thee wed. I am yours, always." He slid the ring over her finger.

Jena's eyes welled up. "I...I am yours, always. I give you this ring as a symbol of my eternal love." She kissed his hand as she put the ring on his finger. "I love you."

The priestess raised her hands to the sky. "Odella, may you bless this union." She smiled. "You may kiss the bride."

As they kissed, his soul touched hers. They were one. "Shall we?"

Jena nodded.

Galin led Jena down the stairs towards the long

tables filled with plates overflowing with food in the middle of the courtyard. They took their place at the head table. Brock, Ellis, and Mae sat down next to them.

"What now?" Ellis asked as he tossed a piece of cornbread in his mouth.

"After Jena and I get back from our honeymoon, the four of us are going north," Galin said.

"North?" Brock asked.

Galin nodded. "Yeah, to get more allies."

"What about them?" Brock asked, pointing at the Feral Orcs.

"They're part of the army now. Treat them as such."

Jena smiled at her new husband. "What's the plan?"

Galin sipped his wine. "Well, we need the strange machines from the gnomes and the wealth of the dwarves to retake Port Eldham and Staerdale Castle." He looked right at Brock. "When we're gone, I need you to contact Sumia. We're going to need their help to win this." He raised his glass. "A toast, to the fall of Staerdale Castle and the Darkstriders."

They all tapped each other's glasses. "Hear, hear!"

"When?" Mae asked.

Galin blinked. For a second, Mae's face became blurry and then it was gone. He must be tired. "Soon, real soon."

THE STORY CONCLUDES **in Full Circle . . .**

Hi, I'm Steven Atwood. I grew up reading fantasy books and watching science fiction whenever I could. When I was young, I played role-playing games within the fantasy genre. Close to the end of my military career, I started to write. It was something I always wanted to do but never did. I write science fiction and fantasy with a fresh perspective.

Visit my website
http://stevenatwood.net

facebook.com/stevenatwoodauthor

twitter.com/SteAtwood

bookbub.com/profile/steven-atwood

instagram.com/steven_atwood_author

<u>Science Fiction</u>

Cyber Invasion

Amari

Nano WMD

<u>Fantasy</u>

Prophecy of Axain Series, 2nd Edition

Prophecy of Axain

Iron Fist Keep

Full Circle

<u>Box Sets</u>

Prophecy of Axain Boxset

www.ingramcontent.com/pod-product-compliance
Lightning Source LLC
Chambersburg PA
CBHW050345190726
48284CB00007BB/2160